The Winged Colt of Casa Mia

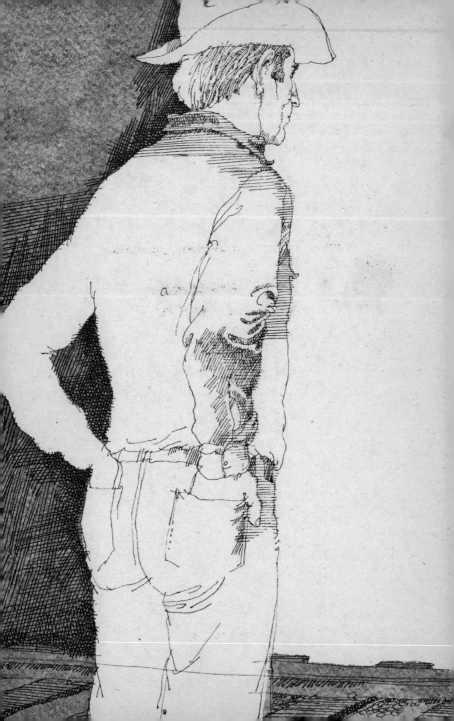

The Winged Colt
of Casa Mia

BETSY BYARS

Illustrated by Richard Cuffari

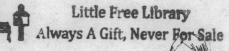

 A CAMELOT BOOK · PUBLISHED BY AVON BOOKS

Other Camelot Books
by Betsy Byars

THE SUMMER OF THE SWANS
THE 18TH EMERGENCY
THE MIDNIGHT FOX

AVON BOOKS
A division of
The Hearst Corporation
959 Eighth Avenue
New York, New York 10019

Text Copyright © 1973 by Betsy Byars.
Illustrations Copyright © 1973 by The Viking Press, Inc.
Published by arrangement with the Viking Press, Inc.
Library of Congress Catalog Card Number: 73-5143.
ISBN 0-380-00201-9

First Camelot Printing, March, 1975.
Second Printing

CAMELOT TRADEMARK REG. U.S. PAT. OFF. AND IN
OTHER COUNTRIES, MARCA REGISTRADA, HECHO EN U.S.A.

Printed in the U.S.A.

Contents

BETSY BYARS was born in Charlotte, North Carolina, and attended Queens College there. After graduation, she worked as a magazine writer, but started writing books as her own children grew. At present she lives in West Virginia with her four children and husband, who is a professor at West Virginia University.

Best in the Business

We stood at the railroad station and looked across the tracks at each other. He was a boy in a dark suit with his hair combed down flat. He was holding a *Mad* magazine. I was a man in dusty boots and dusty pants with a scar down the side of my face that no amount of dust could hide.

I said, "Charles?"

He said, "Uncle Coot? Is that you?"

"Yes."

He tried to grin. "Well, it's me too."

We kept standing there, and then I stepped over to his side of the tracks. Charles was looking up at me, and for a second I could see the Texas sky mirrored in his eyeglasses, the big white clouds. He cleared his throat and said, "I guess you heard I was coming." He started rolling and unrolling his magazine. "Or you wouldn't be here."

"I got your mom's telegram this morning."

"Well, she'll probably send for me in a few weeks or something," he said. "I won't be here forever." He made a tight roll of the *Mad* magazine and held it in his fist.

"Well, sure," I said. "She'll send for you." We stood there a minute more, and then I said, "We might as well stop standing around and get in the truck." We both tried to pick up his suitcase at the same time. Then I got it and carried it over to the truck and we got in.

We drove out of Marfa and neither of us said anything for a mile or two. My truck's old and makes a lot of noise, but it seemed quiet this morning. Once I cleared my throat, and he snapped his head around and asked, "Did you say something?"

"I was just clearing my throat."

"Oh, I thought you said something."

"No." I probably would have said something if I could have thought of anything to say, but I couldn't. We rode on for a few more miles. I was looking straight ahead at the road. He was looking out the window at the mountains. We passed a peak called Devil's Back.

I said, "I reckon this is different from back East where you were in school."

"Yes." We drove another mile or two, and then he said suddenly, "I've seen you in the movies."

I said, "What?" because he had spoken real quiet.

He turned his head toward me. "I've seen you in the *movies*."

"Oh."

There was another silence, and then he said, "I especially remember you in a movie called *Desert Flame*."

"Well, that's over now," I said. Up until this spring I had been in California doing stunts for western movies. I had been doing stunts—or gags, as we call them—the biggest part of my life, and I can tell you that the stunts you see in the movies are real and they are dangerous. There are tricks, of course—fences and barn doors made of soft balsa wood to break easily, ground that's been dug up and softened, rubber hose stirrups—but most of the horse stunts you see are not faked, and stunt horses have to be special animals.

Charles said, "You were riding a white horse."

I said, "Yeah." Then I added again, "But that's over now." I wanted the conversation to end.

"Did the white horse belong to you?"

"Yeah."

"What was his name?"

"Cotton." I tried to make a period of the word. There's a phrase stunt men have about horses—"the best in the business"—and that suited Cotton. In a stunt horse temperament is the important thing, not looks, and I had found Cotton on his way to the slaughterhouse because of a badly wounded leg. There was something about the horse that I liked, and I had taken him and started training him. First I let him fall in a sawdust pit so he would get used to it; then I got him to fall when he was walking, then trotting, and finally to fall in a full gallop, a beautiful fall you've probably seen in a dozen movies.

Maybe you remember the movie *Desert Flame* that Charles was talking about and the scene where the white stallion falls in the desert. That was me and Cotton. I rode Cotton right to the top of a dune, reared him, pretended to take a shot in the shoulder, fell backwards, and me and him rolled head over hoof all the way down that dune without bruising either one of us. Stunt men still talk about that fall sometimes.

"Do you still have that horse?" Charles asked. "I'd like to see him."

"No, I don't have him any more."

"What happened?"

I didn't answer.

"What *happened?*" he asked again.

I said, "Nothing," and began to drive a little faster.

What happened was something I couldn't talk about. That spring Cotton and I had been taking a fall for a movie called *Bright Glory.* The fall wasn't anything special, just a battle scene, and we were to come toward the camera in a full gallop and drop just before we got there. It wasn't anything unusual. Cotton and I had taken that same fall dozens of times with neither of us the worse for it. But this one fall my timing was off. It wasn't off more than a second, but we went down—not in the soft drop area, but beyond it—and crashed into the camera. I got up but Cotton didn't. His front legs were broken.

It took something out of me. Cotton and I had been together for twelve years, and when I knew he was going to have to be shot—I knew it right when I scrambled to my feet in the dust and he didn't—well, I decided then that I wanted to go back home to Texas. The land called me. I wanted to look at the mountains again, to ride through the valleys, to have that bright blinding sky over me. I wanted to be by myself.

The whole thing came back to me as Charles was talking—the accident, the blood from my cheek falling on Cotton's white neck, the pistol shot. I reached up and rubbed the scar on my cheek.

Charles was still talking a mile a minute. "And I remember you jumping across a cliff in *Thunder in Oklahoma*. Remember? You almost didn't make it, and you and the horse just hung there practically on the side of the cliff for a moment."

"Yeah."

"I stayed to see that part of the movie five times and it got better and better. Everybody in the audience held their breath, and some little kids down in front screamed. Was the horse Cotton?"

I nodded.

"I told everybody that was my uncle up there on

the screen—the lady selling popcorn, the man on the aisle, everybody. I don't think half of them believed me. It was the greatest thing I ever saw."

"It wasn't that great, Charles. The cliff wasn't as high as it looked—they had the camera set at an angle so that it looked higher and"—I hesitated—"and I had a horse that made me look good."

"You looked *great*," he said. "The boys at my school wouldn't believe you were my uncle it was so great. They ought to put your name up there with John Wayne's so people would *know*."

He looked at me and his face was shining almost as bright as his glasses. I had never been that great in my life. And at that moment, with the accident still taking up most of my mind, with that one split-second mistake haunting me, the last thing I wanted to hear was how great I was.

"Look, it was just a gag," I said. I was starting to sweat. There was an edge to my voice, but Charles didn't notice.

He said, "And I remember one other time—anyway I thought this was you and I always wanted to ask about it. There was this movie called *Son of* something and—"

"I don't remember all of them," I said.

"But this was such a great stunt you'd *have* to remember. Oh, yeah, it was *Son of Thunderfoot*, and this Indian came riding down a steep hill, and halfway down the hill the horse slipped and—"

"It wasn't me."

"It looked like you and it was a white horse."

"Well, it must have been someone else. There are a lot of stunt men and a lot of white horses. Be quiet so I can drive."

He was still looking at me, squinting through his glasses as if he was looking at a too-bright light. Then he nodded. He turned and started staring out the window. We drove the rest of the way in silence.

The Guy Who Never Got Hurt

There was a cloud of dust behind us as we stopped at the ranch. "Here we are," I said, "Casa Mia." I reached over and opened his door for him. Beyond, the buildings looked old and dusty in the bright sunlight.

Charles didn't say anything. He got out of the truck and went into the house with his suitcase. In about five minutes he came out in a pair of blue jeans so new the stiffness was still in them.

I was at the corral saddling up Clay. I wanted to get off by myself for a while, because just talking about Cotton had brought back my loss. Charles spotted me and came over.

He stuck his hands down into his jeans pockets kind of casual-like, and then he pulled out a little square of paper that said his pants had been inspected by Number 28. He crumpled the paper and looked at me.

I said, "Listen, Charles, I got to go off for an hour or two and—"

He said, "I'd like to learn how to ride a horse now." His eyeglasses looked like they had been bought a couple of sizes too big so he could grow into them.

I said, "Well, sure, Charles, you can learn to ride if you want, but if you're going to be here for a few weeks there'll be plenty of time."

"I've seen it done a thousand times," he said.

"Yeah, but seeing it done isn't doing it. Look, why don't you finish reading your magazine or something for a couple of hours. You can unpack. I've got to—"

"I've read four complete books on horsemanship, including the *Encyclopedia of Horses*, both volumes. Have you ever read that?"

"Well, no, but—"

"I even memorized the ten rules of good horsemanship. One: A good horseman controls the horse with his hands, legs, and the weight of his body. Those are called the aids, Uncle Coot."

"Oh."

"The most important aid is the legs. You use them to teach the horse to move. If you press the horse with your left leg, the horse moves to the left. If you press the horse . . ."

By this time I could see that nothing was going to satisfy him but getting up on a horse and trying out those aids. I gave up on getting off by myself for the moment. "I'll saddle Stump for you," I said.

He stopped talking and blinked his eyes. "Stump? That's a funny name for a horse."

"Not this horse."

I started into the barn and he followed. "Why, Uncle Coot?"

"You know what a stump does, don't you?"

"Well, nothing."

"Same with this horse."

Old Stump was a twenty-year-old horse that was known far and wide for not moving. That horse could outstand a tree. He used to be in the movies every now and then when a studio call would come for a horse that would stand without moving—like when a cowboy had to leap off a saloon roof or a balcony onto a horse, because for a gag like that you have to have a horse that won't move. A stunt man can get crippled if he lands on a western saddle just a few inches out of position—and Stump wouldn't move an inch. He would stand for hours with his head down, looking at something on the ground, and you could saddle him and spur him and holler yourself hoarse, and he would still stand there contemplating the ground.

We took the saddle out to him—I knew there wasn't any sense calling him over to us—and all the way Charles was quoting things out of the *Encyclopedia of Horses*. He went on about it so much that by the time we got to Stump I had heard just about all I cared to about horsemanship.

I saddled Stump and gave Charles a boost, and he got in the saddle without too much trouble. Then right away he said, "I think the saddle is set too far back. It's very important for the saddle to be in the right position."

"It's fine," I said. "It just feels that way because—"

He didn't let me finish. He threw his leg over and sat sideways on the saddle, getting ready, I reckon, to jump down. "The *Encyclopedia* says that the saddle" —he started, but that was as far as he got because right then Stump started to move.

I wouldn't have believed it if I hadn't been right there because that horse hated to move. To this day I don't know what caused it. You would think that a horse who would stand still when a hundred-and-eighty-pound man landed on his back wouldn't mind a kid sitting sideways on him for a minute or two, but Stump did.

Stump stopped looking at the ground. He tossed his head, jerked around, and took a couple of sidesteps. There's nothing gives a new rider a worse feeling than when his horse starts going sideways.

Charles squealed in a high voice, which wasn't one of anybody's rules of good horsemanship, and held on to the saddle with both hands. He got ready to slide off, only Stump came around real quick, kind of dipped under him, and Charles's leg went over the horse and—I was as surprised as he was—he ended up facing backwards.

I've done some backwards riding myself in rodeos, and I tell you it gives you a funny feeling the first

time you try it. Charles squealed again and reached out for something to hold, only there wasn't anything there but Stump's tail. As soon as I saw him grab that, I knew he'd made a mistake.

Stump put his head down then and began to double buck, which is jumping up in the air like a goat, hitting the ground, and leaping again. Charles went with him—right up in the air with his arms and legs leaving the horse. I could see the sky between the horse and the boy, but then every single time Charles came right down on Stump again. It would have been a blessing for him to go ahead and get thrown, only he couldn't seem to do it.

Then Stump started hitting the ground with his legs as stiff as posts and his back legs kicking out be-

hind like a mule's. I ran after him, but before I could get to him, he started going around the corral backwards, twisting and turning. Then he finished by throwing himself down on his side, with Charles's left leg underneath. It worried me for a minute, because a man can break a leg getting jabbed by a stirrup after hitting the ground. That's why stunt men use a rubber hose stirrup on the left side.

I don't know what the *Encyclopedia* had to say about that situation, but I hollered, "Get off, boy!" and Charles dragged his leg out from under Stump and scrambled out of the way, not hurt at all.

He kept going until he was on the other side of the corral fence. Then he stood there looking at Stump on the ground. After a minute he said, "Is he dead?"

"Stump? No."

"But he's just lying there."

"He'll get up in a minute. That's the first exercise he's had in fifteen years." The air went out of Charles then, and he looked smaller than ever. I said, "Let's get back to the house."

We started walking, him limping and me walking about the same way because of an old hip injury I got in a movie called *Guns of Navaho* that never bothers me in the saddle, only when I walk a distance. So we limped along, and I tried to think of something nice to say. Finally I said, "You really stayed on that horse though."

"I thought I never would get thrown."

"Me too."

"Actually I *wanted* to be thrown." He hung his head and said, "It probably seemed very funny to you."

"No, it didn't seem funny."

"I mean, you being such a great rider and all. I've seen you in the movies and I *know*."

"Charles, didn't you ever get on a horse before?" I asked, changing the subject.

"No."

"Didn't your mom ever—"

"*No*." We took a few more steps and he said, "Actually I haven't seen much of my mother." His mom, my sister Jean, was the greatest trick rider I ever saw but not much of a mother. She had put Charles in school in the East—I guess more to get him out of the way than anything else—and then a month ago she had broken her shoulder in a rodeo in Phoenix. Money was scarce after that, and so she had sent Charles to me. She had said in her telegram it would be for a couple of months. Charles had said a couple of weeks. Knowing my sister, I was afraid the boy was here to stay.

"Well, that's the way Jean always was," I said finally. "Looks like at least she would have taught you to ride a horse."

He stopped then—we were almost to the steps— and he put one hand on my arm. Behind his dusty eyeglasses his eyes were very bright. He said, "But I'll learn. I'm going to be just like you."

He kept looking at me, and I suddenly realized that all he knew about me he had learned from the movie screen. I was the man who did the impossible. I was the big hero, the guy who could leap cliffs, cross roaring streams, take forty-foot jumps into lakes, and fall a hundred times without hardly getting dusty. I was the guy who never got hurt.

And while I was standing there, trying to think of something to say, something that would show him what I really was, the lady came up and told us about the colt with wings.

Something Wrong
at the Minneys'

This lady, Mrs. Minney, was another unexpected thing
that had happened that spring. She and her husband
had come to Texas from New York and had bought an
old worn-down place across the road. They had come,
Mrs. Minney told me, because she was writing a book
about the cliff dwellers who used to live in the mountains around here, and she wanted to investigate the
caves. Her husband was an artist who was tired of
painting buildings and subways and was going to paint
horses and cattle and mountains for a change. The
Minneys had had a good bit of trouble getting settled
because neither of them was a practical person. I don't
think a day went by without Mrs. Minney's driving
over in her truck to ask me about one thing or another.
As soon as I saw her coming, I said to Charles, "Well,
something's wrong at the Minneys' again."

He turned his head to watch the truck. "Who are the Minneys?"

"That's Mrs. Minney coming now—the smartest woman I ever met to be so dumb."

Mrs. Minney stopped her truck and got out. Her shirttail was flapping, and her hair was rising, and she came running over so fast Charles and I backed up a few steps. Even when she came to a halt, she still seemed to be going somewhere.

I said politely, "Mrs. Minney, this is my nephew Charles."

She said, "Mr. Cutter! Mr. Cutter! Do you know anything about cutting the wings off a colt?"

I said, "*What?*"

She repeated it. "Do you know anything about cutting the wings off a colt?"

I just stood there. I thought about this old Appaloosa I used to have with a map of Mexico on his side. It was my first stunt horse, and he could take as good a fall as you ever saw. And then one day—I hadn't had Mex a year when this happened—when we got ready to fall he just planted his feet and braced his neck and *stood*. I couldn't believe it. I knew Mex was telling me he was never going to fall again, but my mind couldn't take it in. Now Mrs. Minney had brought me up short in the same way.

"What?"

She sighed. "Wings! Little wings about that long on either side of his shoulders." She shook her head.

"I just don't know what to do about it. I've never seen a colt with wings before."

"I haven't either, Mrs. Minney," I said. "But whatever those things turn out to be, I can assure you that they won't be wings."

"Why not?"

"Because they *couldn't* be."

She looked at me closer. I must have had an amused look on my face, because she said, "This is no joking matter, Mr. Cutter. I told you when we bought the mare that we wanted her and the colt for the grandchildren. I trusted you not to sell me a horse that was going to have a colt with anything extra."

I lowered my voice, the way I do when I'm trying to calm an excited animal. "Mrs. Minney, I believe there's just been a little mistake here."

You can soothe a horse with your voice sometimes, but not Mrs. Minney. She got louder. "If there's been a mistake, it's yours for thinking I'm going to stand for this."

"Now, Mrs. Minney—"

"I tell you I am *frantic*. I went out this morning to load my truck, and there was the colt. It had been born during the night, and while I was standing there with my heart in my throat—there is nothing as moving as new life—well, then I saw the wings. And I tell you I haven't been the same since. Frank has been in the bedroom with the shades drawn. With his sensitive nature he's not even able to paint."

"Mrs. Minney, there is no such thing as a horse with wings. There never has been and never will be."

"But there *could* be," Charles said. His eyes had gotten big with interest. He stepped right in front of Mrs. Minney. All his aches and pains seemed forgotten.

I said calmly, "I beg your pardon, Charles, but I have seen horses and known horses since the day I was born. And there never has been such a thing as a horse with wings."

"There's a vase from Mycenae—it's in the National Museum in Greece—and there's a winged horse on it. Some people say that it's a scene from mythology, but others, including me, believe that there actually *was* a winged horse and—"

"Charles!"

"And then there are the horses from Pech Merle —that's a cave in France," he continued in a rush.

"I am familiar with that cave," Mrs. Minney said. I could see that she was far more impressed with Charles's knowledge of horses than with mine.

"And there are horses painted on the wall"— Charles went on—"and above the horses are hand-shaped marks like wings."

"That's true!" Mrs. Minney said. "I never thought of it, but those marks *are* like wings."

"And do you remember the skeleton found in the diggings at—"

"*Charles!*" He shut up long enough for me to say, "Now that is enough! Mrs. Minney doesn't want to hear you trying to prove something that is impossible."

"I do," Mrs. Minney cried.

I ignored her. "Mrs. Minney is worried enough without your adding to it. She doesn't care what's been painted on vases and cave walls and—"

"I do!" Mrs. Minney cried again.

"No, you don't!" She stepped back for a moment. "What the three of us are interested in right now"— I continued as calmly as I could—"is what has been on this earth, actually been on this earth. And there has never been a horse with wings and never will be. Never!"

They both looked at me without speaking. Then Mrs. Minney sat down on the porch steps. She said, "Well, actually, it is a relief, Mr. Cutter, to hear that." She sighed and patted her face with her shirttail. "Nobody knows what a relief it is to think you have a horse with wings and then find out you have a horse with—" She broke off and looked at me. "What would it be that the horse has?"

I did not want her to get excited again so I said, calmly, "Well, since it's not wings, it will have to be something else. I think we can all agree on that." I glanced from Mrs. Minney to Charles.

"Well, if it's *not* wings," Charles said, "then of course it *will* have to be something else, but I still think—"

I rested my hand on his shoulder so firmly that he choked down the rest of his words. "What I am going to do, Mrs. Minney," I continued, "is come over to your place now, look at the colt, and tell you what he has."

"Could I come too, Mrs. Minney?" Charles asked, "I'd like to see this for myself. It is quite possible, you know, that this is the first winged colt in the—"

"Charles!"

"Of course you come." Mrs. Minney took a deep breath and sighed. "I feel better now. My trouble is that I get excited too easily. Another woman, seeing she had a colt with wings, would probably have the wings removed in a sensible way and go about her business."

We climbed into the truck, and she said, "The trouble is that all I can think about just now is investigating the caves, and when something happens to distract me, I get upset."

"Your reaction seems normal to me," Charles said. "A colt with wings would be exciting and upsetting to anybody."

I nudged Charles and said to Mrs. Minney, "Anyway, everything's going to be all right *now*."

Mrs. Minney backed the truck around and almost went in the ditch. Then she said, "Yes, we'll look at the colt, find out what the trouble is, and then go in the house and have some lemonade. Would you like that?"

"I would," Charles said.

"And tomorrow I'll be back at work. You cannot imagine what excitement there is in entering a cave where men lived hundreds of years ago and finding bits of sandals and bows and arrows. Even a bit of pollen centuries old can tell what plants these men had. A piece of bone can tell what diseases they suffered from. You, young man, with your knowledge of caves, probably know something about this already. You"—she leaned forward and looked at me—"probably don't."

"No'm."

She drove for a few minutes. Then she shook her head and said, "Still and all, I will feel easier in my mind when I know what those things on the colt are."

I thought I heard Charles say "Wings" under his breath. I wasn't sure, but I nudged him again anyway. That kept him quiet for the rest of the drive.

A Surprise

We stopped in front of the barn and got out. Mr. Minney stuck his head out the back window of the house, and Mrs. Minney called to him, "Don't worry, Frank, those aren't wings on the colt after all."

"They looked like wings to me," he called back.

"Mr. Cutter says no."

"What are they then, Mr. Cutter?" he asked, still leaning out the window.

"I'll let you know in a minute." I took off my hat and waved it at him. This was a thing I used to do in the rodeo. It always seemed to give the crowd a lot of confidence in what I was about to do, but not Mr. and Mrs. Minney.

Mrs. Minney waited without speaking until my hat was back on my head, and then she said, "Frank and I don't like this, Mr. Cutter. We don't like it at all."

"Yeah, I got that feeling, Mrs. Minney."

"We had such happy visions of the grandchildren riding around the ranch. Come on in the barn." She took me and Charles in an iron grip and led us down to the last stall. We stood there for a moment because it took our eyes a while to see in the dim barn.

Peggy, the mare, was a fine chestnut with a white mane and tail. I reached over and scratched her muzzle and said, "Good girl." I couldn't see the colt— nothing but the spindly legs because he was on the other side of his mother, drinking her milk. Then Peggy shifted to the side, and there was the prettiest little Palomino colt you ever saw. The sun was coming through the window behind us, and it shone down on the colt. He was pale gold like wheat, and his mane and tail were silver. There was a white spot on his forehead.

As I watched he moved closer to his mother on his long awkward legs. I said, "Why, there's nothing wrong with that colt. Look at him, Charles. He's perfect."

"You're not going to get away with that," Mrs. Minney said. "There's something wrong and I know it. And don't think for a minute that you're going to give me a few comforting phrases and walk out of this barn like you're not responsible."

I leaned forward and looked again. "There are no wings on that colt."

Right when I was saying that in a loud voice, the colt gave a little sidestep, nuzzled up against his mother, and kind of lost his balance. That was when something came fluttering out from his sides. It was a quick movement, so light and fast I almost didn't see it.

"I'd like to know what you call those," Mrs. Minney said in a hard voice.

"Wings," Charles said.

I said, "Now hold on a minute. Horses don't have wings. That is a known fact."

"This one does," Charles said in a voice hushed with excitement. He turned and looked at me. His whole face was lit up.

For a minute I had a funny falling sensation. Like one time when I jumped a horse off a forty-foot cliff into a Missouri lake. When I jumped I was so scared I had a knot in my stomach as big as a cannon ball, and I thought that cannon ball would probably take me all the way to the bottom of the lake. I never made a jump like that again.

Charles turned to Mrs. Minney. "Did you notice the shape of the wings, Mrs. Minney? They seem to have the same structure as those of the newborn swift and may never be really strong enough for flight."

"I'm glad to see there's at least one person with brains in the Cutter family," Mrs. Minney said.

"On the other hand," Charles continued, "the wings could increase in strength until they are quite capable of lifting the weight of horse and rider, which I estimate to be about fifteen hundred pounds."

"The boy knows more about horses than a lot of other people in this barn," Mrs. Minney said coldly. She had been a city lady for so long that she still carried over her shoulder a big leather pocketbook. Now she kind of struck me with it so there wouldn't be any doubt who it was that didn't know much about horses.

"Mrs. Minney, listen, I am just as surprised as you are. There *is* an explanation for this though. I do know that." The cannon ball in my stomach was so heavy I thought it was going to bring me down to my knees in the barn.

"Huh!"

"A perfectly logical and sensible explanation."

"Ho!"

"I've been working with animals all my life, and I know there is always a logical and sensible explanation for everything."

Without giving me a chance to try to think up this explanation, she nudged me again with her pocketbook. I said, "All right, Mrs. Minney, if you'll just calm down a minute, I will step into the stall and have a look at the colt and find out what has happened."

"I think I already know what has happened," Charles said eagerly.

Mrs. Minney folded her arms in front of her. "I think we *all* know what has happened," she said. "Only one of us is too stubborn to admit it."

"What occurs to me," Charles went on, "is that this could be a throwback in the gene structure. Or perhaps the result of some drug that the mare took during the gestation period. Uncle Coot, did you give the mare any drugs?"

"No."

"Did she have access to any strange foods?"

"Will you hush and let me try to find out what has really happened here?"

I opened the door of the stall, went in, and rubbed Peggy's neck. You have to move gently with a colt that's a few hours old. I usually try to handle them from birth to get them used to me. I knelt down and ran my hands over the colt. I turned to see him in a better light. Now the wings were the most obvious things in the world. I couldn't understand why I hadn't seen them earlier.

"Well?" Mrs. Minney said.

I put my hands on the colt's sides, and the wings came out and fluttered against my hands. I couldn't say anything because I felt like I had a wad of cotton rammed down my throat. I stood up slowly.

"Well?" Mrs. Minney said, louder.

I took off my hat and ran my hand over my hair. I shifted my pants up an inch or two and jammed my hands in my back pockets. I looked down at the colt and still I couldn't speak.

"Well?"

"Mrs. Minney." I swallowed and the sound of it was like a gun going off in the quiet barn. "Mrs. Minney, I don't know why and I don't know how, but you have got a colt with wings."

Texas Pegasus

As soon as I said that, Mrs. Minney took the leather pocketbook and brought it down hard on my head. It was like getting hit with a saddle. Then she started saying, "I knew it, I knew it," and "You're not getting away with this. You're not, you're not, you're *not*." I never saw such a mad woman in my life.

"Mrs. Minney, Mrs. Minney, ma'am, wait a minute. Listen!" I was trying to get out of the stall without upsetting Peggy and the colt and to shield my head at the same time. Mrs. Minney drew back and watched me. Her eyes were such little slits I couldn't even see what color they were. "Now, *listen*," I cried again.

"I'm listening," she said, taking a deep breath, "but it better be good."

"I just don't think you realize what you have

here, Mrs. Minney, that's all I want to say. A horse with wings is a valuable thing. If you have the only winged horse in the country, in the world actually, then you've really got something." She didn't look impressed. "A winged pig would even be great, a winged squirrel, but a *winged horse!*"

"Actually there really are winged squirrels," Charles said, "only the wings are more like folds of skin."

"Will you shut up, Charles?"

"I just thought you'd want to know about the flying squirrels."

"Thank you."

Charles said, "And there are also flying lizards in

Indonesia, but actually they only glide from tree to tree, and there is also some kind of creature called a flying fox, but I believe—"

"That's enough, Charles! Mrs. Minney is upset enough without your alarming her even more with these wild stories of flying foxes and lizards."

"The thought of flying lizards in Indonesia is much less alarming to me," Mrs. Minney said, "than what is happening here in this barn now."

"Well, sure," I said. "I never worried about those lizards much over there either."

"You never even *knew* about those lizards!" She wasn't going to let me get away with a thing.

I said in a firm voice, "The point is, Mrs. Minney, that this colt is quite possibly the most valuable colt that has ever been born."

"All I want—" she said. And she opened her eyes wide enough for me to see what color they were. They were a cold gray. "All I *wanted* was a horse that I could sit on and ride when I felt like it and that my grandchildren could sit on and ride when they came out to visit."

"I know, but this—"

"And if you think we are going to get on any horse with wings, you are mistaken." She leaned forward and looked at me real close. I had a horse named Bumble Bee used to do that before she bit. "If it's got wings," she said, "then it just might *fly!*" She pulled back and looked at me with her arms folded over her pocketbook.

"Mrs. Minney," I said, "what is it you want me to do? Whatever it is—just tell me and I'll do it."

"That's more like it," she said. "I want one of two things. Either you remove those wings and leave no trace they were there—and frankly I don't think you can do that—or you take the mare and the colt back and refund my money."

"It's my duty," Charles said, "to tell you that this time, Mrs. Minney, my uncle happens to be right. A horse with wings is valuable. The public is always eager to see something unusual and—"

Mrs. Minney put her hands on her hips. "I thought better of you, young man, than that. If what you are suggesting is that I run some sort of carnival side show and exhibit this poor unfortunate animal— Why, I'd as soon turn babies out of their carriages."

"I wasn't suggesting a carnival exactly, but television appearances would be a possibility. You could become famous."

"What do I care for fame? What is fame except people recognizing you, and everybody I want to recognize me does so already."

"But I mean really famous, *world* famous."

"Young man, if you become famous because of something you have done, that is one thing. Becoming famous because of something you *own* is another matter. Now I don't want to hear another word." She turned to me. "Are you taking the colt and mare back or not?"

I looked down at the little Palomino nuzzling

against his mother. I wanted the colt all right. I wanted him a lot. I don't guess a man can be a stunt man for half his life and not want a winged colt.

"Well?" she said.

"I would be pleased to take the colt and mare back."

"And no *forcing* this animal to fly either," she said. "I don't want to turn on my television some night and see you forcing him to fly."

"No'm."

"I want you to be good to this horse. He'll fly if he wants to."

"Yes'm."

"Shake on it."

I put out my hand and we shook. Then she got a firmer grip on my hand and leaned over and said, "And there better not be any tricks."

"There won't be."

Charles and I took a last look at the colt, and then the three of us went out of the barn. Mr. Minney was still leaning out the back window. I tried to pretend I didn't see him and kept walking, but he called, "Mr. Cutter! Mr. Cutter!" I kept walking and he called, "Mr. Cutter, did you find out what those things were?" I kept walking. "The things we thought were wings—what are they?"

"Mr. Minney's calling you," Charles said. "He wants to know what—"

"I heard him." I shifted my hat and said in a low voice, "They're wings, Mr. Minney."

"What?" Mr. Minney called.

"*Wings!*" I shouted. "*Wings!*"

"But I thought you said—"

"He was *wrong*," Mrs. Minney said behind me. She sounded real satisfied.

We hesitated a minute, but she didn't say anything about the lemonade or driving us home in the truck, so Charles and I began walking. I was too stunned to talk, but Charles plowed right in.

"You know, I thought of something else," he said. "There's a statue in one of the French museums of a horse with wings and also—"

"There is no such thing as a colt with wings," was all I could manage to say.

"Also there was Pegasus—he was the most famous flying horse in the world—and do you know how they tamed him, Uncle Coot?"

"There is no such thing as a—"

"With a golden bridle. And I also remember reading an article in *Time* magazine about this man who believes that Greek myths like Pegasus really did exist, that they were super beings from other planets. So maybe there *was* a winged colt at one time, and this colt is a descendant!"

"There is no such thing as—"

"And there's another statue—I think it's Egyptian—and—" Charles kept talking about flying horses all the way to the ranch. I thought he never would run out of things to say. I thought he must have spent the biggest part of his life reading books. Finally I interrupted and said, "Wait a minute. How do you know all this stuff, Charles?"

"I read."

"Well, yeah, sure, everybody reads, but they don't know all that stuff."

"Well, I read a lot. I once decided to read every book in the school library—that was because I had a lot of extra time, you know, like during vacations when everyone else had gone home?" He looked up at me. "But anyway, getting back to the statues, if there *was* no such thing as a flying horse, well, then why doesn't *one* of those countries have a flying bear or a flying dog? You never see statues of flying dogs."

"I don't know, Charles. The only place I ever saw anything about a horse with wings was on a gas station sign, and I can't even remember which one it was now." The truth was I was starting to feel dazed. It was like the time I did a gag for a movie called *Riders of the Plain*. They tied this rope around my chest, and it was about two hundred feet long and six men were holding the other end of the rope. Well, I got on my horse and started out, full gallop, until the rope was played out, and then I was yanked backward from the saddle. It was supposed to look like a blow from a rifle had knocked me from my horse. It doesn't sound like a bad gag—I'd done worse—but when I slammed into the ground, my knee rammed into my forehead. I wandered around for the rest of the day feeling dazed and stupid. That was the same way I felt now. I had seen that colt. I had looked right at him. The wings had touched my hands. I still couldn't take it in.

"I wish," Charles was saying, "that I was close to a really good research library, because I would like to look into this matter in my spare time." He stumbled in his excitement. "Hey, you know what I'm going to do? I'm going to start a record of the colt and keep notes on everything he does. Tomorrow I'll take pictures with my Polaroid and—what time can we get the colt?"

"Afternoon."

"He'll be walking by then?" He looked up at me. His eyes were as round as quarters.

"He'll be walking," I said. "He may even be flying."

And Charles leaped up in the air and hollered, "Yeah!" I guess I would have joined him if it hadn't been for my hip. I resettled my hat and kept walking.

After a minute Charles said, "Oh, yeah, Uncle Coot, I just thought of something else. There's this Etruscan vase—it was dug up near Cerveteri—and on this vase is a wonderful flying horse. It—"

The Storm
That Went On and On

We got home with the colt the next day, and I began to realize right then that my past experience with horses wasn't going to help me as much as I'd thought.

This colt was different. It wasn't just his wings. It was something in his nature, something that made him shyer, less predictable than other colts. And he was lightning quick. It took me the best part of two days to ease a light halter on him, and after two weeks I was still trying to teach him to back up on command.

All this time Charles was writing down everything the colt did in a notebook. I never saw anybody write so much. It wasn't the kind of thing a person would casually take down about an animal, but real scientific things, measurements and behavior and all.

I was in the notebook too. Everything I tried with

the colt during those first weeks was written down. And if I'd stop for a minute he'd say, "How're you doing, Uncle Coot? Is anything wrong?"

I'd shake my head. "Nothing more than usual, Charles."

"What do you mean?"

"I just mean that it's not going to be as easy to train Alado as you're thinking." Alado was what Charles had named the colt because *alado* means "winged" in Spanish.

"Oh, I know it's not going to be easy, but you can do it. You've already haltered him."

"Yeah, but it's almost like working with a different kind of animal, Charles, it's—"

"I know, Uncle Coot. That's why it's so lucky that you're the one training him. Nobody else could do it."

"Yeah." And I'd hear him click his ballpoint pen so he'd be ready to write down what I tried next.

Those first weeks had a strangeness about them. There is something about a new and unknown horse that usually brings up the spirit in a man. When I was a boy there were wild horses on the range, and there was something about seeing an untamed horse tossing its mane and running like the wind—didn't matter if it was a shining black, a great mustang, or a flea-bitten pinto—that made the blood rise in me, that made me feel free and wild too, even though I was nothing but a skinny, patched-pants boy.

I should have felt that way even more about

Alado, because he was wild and free in a way that I had never imagined, but I didn't. I felt about the colt the same way I had felt about the boy when he turned to me that first day with his face shining and said, "I want to be just like you." It was a sort of worried, uneasy feeling, as if something was going to happen that I couldn't control.

It showed in the pictures we took with Charles's Polaroid. I had a stiff, strained look. The colt was a pale unnatural blur. And Charles looked like a kid who had just discovered Christmas. To look at those pictures, you would know that there was going to be trouble, and the trouble came in August with as bad a storm as I ever saw.

Southwest Texas has always had a lot of storms. I remember when I was a boy there was one so bad that my grandad lost five head of cattle and two horses on the range in one afternoon. The lightning just seems to pour down from the sky like arrows, hitting whatever's in the open. And I remember that afternoon my grandad got so mad that he stood up and hollered, "All right, lightning, go ahead and strike me and the boy too and be done with it. Go ahead! Strike us!" It scared me, standing there beside him, and one time later when I did get hit by lightning on the range—got thrown out of the saddle and came to lying on the ground with my mouth filling with rain water—the first thing I thought of was my grandad yelling at the lightning.

The horses were restless that afternoon, sensing

that a storm was coming. The air was so full of electricity that little balls of electricity like peas were flashing on their ears and tails.

Late in the day the horses came up closer to the house, stood in a restless bunch for a while, and ran away. Then they came back and did the whole thing again.

"Shouldn't we do something?" Charles asked in a worried voice.

These storms make me as uneasy as the horses because weather out here is usually an excess. If it rains, it can rain six inches in one hour; or if it's dry, there won't be a drop of rain for two months; or if it's hailing, balls of hail will make dents in trucks and raise knots on people's heads. There just doesn't seem to be such a thing as a gentle storm in southwest Texas.

"Nothing we can do," I said.

He looked to the horizon, which was black and streaked with lightning. Then he looked at the horses moving nervously around the corral, pawing at the ground, running in spurts.

Alado was the worst. He would run first this way, pause to listen, then run the other way. The rumblings of thunder caused his ears to flatten against his head and he tossed his mane in the air again and again. The sound of thunder doubles over the mountains and rumbles down twice as loud as you ever heard it anywhere else.

"My main worry," Charles said finally, "is the colt."

"The colt's all right. He's with his ma and they've got a shelter."

"But, Uncle Coot—"

"These horses stay out on the range all winter. They can take care of themselves."

"But—"

"They're all right."

We went into the house and had a supper of fried beans and bread. Charles didn't do more than push his beans around on his plate. "I've heard of lightning striking animals," he said finally in a low voice.

"It'll do that occasionally," I admitted.

"And one stroke of lightning can measure more than fifteen million volts."

"I guess. I never measured one."

He didn't say anything else for a minute, and I thought that the trouble with him was that he knew too much for his own good. He got up, pushed his plate away, and went to the window. If the horses were close to the house he could see them from there. I watched him leaning against the glass. Then he looked down at his hands and said what he had been working up to all along. "We could bring the colt into the house."

It was only seven o'clock now, but black as night. Everything was still. The wind hadn't started to blow yet, and for the moment there was no thunder either.

"I think Alado's all alone by the fence. I think all the other horses are in the shelter." He turned around and started stammering, "Uncle Coot, please! I know

I'm not supposed to bother you. Mom told me how you hate to be bothered, but if you'll just do this one thing I'll never ask you for anything again. I'll stay completely out of your way. You won't even know I'm around."

"Now, hold on, Charles. Be sensible."

"I *am* being sensible. The colt's not like any of the others. He's got wings and if the wind gets strong enough—well, anything could happen. He's *got* to come in the house."

I could see that he wasn't going to be able to sleep a wink with the colt out in the storm. I didn't imagine I'd sleep too well myself. I said, "All right, I'll get the colt."

It was a mistake and I knew it, but I pulled on my poncho, yanked my hat down on my head, and started out the door. "You stay here though. Understand?"

"I will, and thank you very, very much."

"Just stay here."

"Yes sir, and I promise I will never, ever be any trouble to you again as long as I live."

He would have promised anything to get me out the door. He was all but pushing me. I stepped out onto the porch, and right then the lightning struck somewhere to the west. I was ready to turn and go back into the house. If I'd had good sense I would have. Only I looked back at Charles in the doorway, and I stepped off the porch and ran for the corral.

The wind came up as I got halfway across the yard. It came up quick and strong at my back and doubled me over. I ran in a crouch to the corral. I couldn't see the horses anywhere, but I started struggling to get the gate open against the wind.

Right then there was another crash of lightning. This one had a human sound. It was like somebody had screamed in my ear, and I felt like somebody had hit me on the head with a sledge hammer at the same time. The pain went all the way through me, down to my toes, and then I blacked out.

When I came to, I was crumpled up against the fence like a piece of uprooted weed. In a movie called *Six Outlaws* I was once thrown right through a balsa wood fence. It was so real-looking that when the movie was shown, people in the audience would let out a moan when I went through that fence. It was nothing, though, I can tell you, compared to slamming into this real fence. Every bone in my body hurt.

I tried to get to my feet by holding on to the fence post, but my legs and arms were like rope, and my head must have weighed a hundred pounds. Finally I gave up and slumped to the ground and bent my head over my trembling knees.

The storm lasted for another hour. There was a hard blistering rain and deadly lightning and wind and some hail thrown in for good measure. I just lay there. I couldn't do anything but pull my poncho over my head to keep the worst of it off my face and wait. I didn't know then, and I still don't, whether it was getting hit by lightning or being slammed against the fence that shook me up. Whatever the cause, I was in bad shape.

After a bit the rain slackened, and Charles came running out with a black umbrella he had brought with him from school. The wind tore it out of his hand first thing and tumbled it out of sight. He ran over to where I was, zigzagging in the wind. He looked so frail I half expected him to go blowing away after the umbrella.

"Are you all right?" he hollered, bending over me.

I couldn't do more than nod.

"Where's Alado?" He was looking over the fence now, trying to see where the horses were.

I reached out and grabbed him, and he helped me to my feet. It was hard getting to the house with him looking backwards the whole way. But we finally made it, and I sank down on my bunk.

"I'll get you some dry clothes," Charles said, but I shook my head. He hesitated and then covered me up with a blanket.

"Did you see Alado out there anywhere?" he asked in a worried voice, tucking the blanket around my shoulders.

I shook my head.

"Do you think he's in the shelter?"

I nodded.

"Do you think you'll feel like going out in a little while and making sure he's all right?" Before I could shake my head there was the sound of the wind getting stronger. Charles glanced toward the door. "I think another storm's coming."

It was the last thing I heard because I closed my eyes and fell asleep. When I woke up it was dawn. Charles was slumped over by the window, his face on the sill.

He woke up as soon as I stirred and came over. "How are you this morning, Uncle Coot?"

"Well, I'm better," I said. "A little sore and stiff maybe." Actually I was like a board. If I bent, I would most probably break.

"It's my fault," he said, looking down at his feet.

"Well, let's don't get into that." The last thing I wanted right then was an argument about whose fault my condition was.

"No, it *is* my fault," he continued. "I thought about it all night. Anybody else but you would probably have been killed."

"Yeah." I was just too tired and sore to argue. I got up, moved my arms a little, and shook my legs. I expected my hip to be hurting more than anything else because that's my weak spot. Instead it was my shoulders. I started over to the dresser, moving real slow, to get some clothes, and when I passed the window I stopped and looked out.

In the pale light of dawn the whole place had a strange look. Water was still lying on the ground because too much rain had fallen to be taken into the earth, and everything had a faded, colorless look. On the horizon the huge orange sun was just coming into view.

Charles came and stood by me and said, "I don't see the horses." He grabbed my arm in both his hands and yanked. "I don't see the horses!"

"Now, don't get upset." I limped out on the porch and stood at the edge of the steps. Charles came out and grabbed my arm again.

I said quickly, "Don't yank my arm, Charles, because my shoulders are—"

"Where's the *colt*, Uncle Coot?" he asked, yanking my arm harder. His voice broke and I thought my shoulder had too. "Where's Alado?"

The Search That Didn't Go On Long Enough

A person can see for miles from my front porch, but the only horse in sight this morning was Stump. He was standing about a hundred yards from the fence looking at a puddle on the ground.

"Where could the horses be?" Charles asked in a funny voice. The gate had blown off its hinges during one of the storms, and I figured the horses had left some time during the night.

"Now, don't go getting upset."

"I can't help it. They're gone." He looked at me. "Alado's gone."

"I can see that."

"Well, what are you going to do?"

I sighed, and even that hurt my shoulders. "What I'll do is ride out this morning and find them." I made it sound easier than it was. In my condition even lifting the saddle wasn't going to be a cinch.

"I'll go too," Charles said.

"Charles, look, I think you'd be better off staying here."

"But I want to go. I want to help."

"I know that." The plain truth was that Charles hadn't caught on to riding. He'd tried—I'll give him that—but he just hadn't gotten the hang of it. He was always yelling proudly, "Look at me, Uncle Coot," and I'd look just in time to see him bounce out of the saddle or something.

I said, "Well, Charles, I'd like your company, but there's only one horse and that's Stump, and—"

"I could ride behind you."

"—and I'd make better time alone."

He ducked his head and said, "Oh, well sure. I should have thought of that."

"Let's get some breakfast."

I went into the house, changed my clothes, and scrambled some eggs. We ate without saying anything. Charles kept getting up from the table and going to the window to see if the horses had come back. I don't think a bite of food went into his mouth the whole meal.

After breakfast I saddled Stump, mounted, and sat there. For the first time I knew how that horse felt, because right then I could have sat in the saddle looking down at the ground for about ten hours, not moving once.

"Good luck, Uncle Coot," Charles called. He was on the porch, watching us with one arm wrapped around the post.

"Right." I finally got Stump to take a few steps. "Good luck!"

I nodded to him—I would have waved if I could have—and very slowly Stump and I set off.

There's something about this land that always stays the same. I thought about that as I rode. A lot has happened here. A lot of people have come and gone—Mexicans, traders, Comanches, ranchers, outlaws—but they didn't change the land. It's just too big, I guess, too hard. It's the kind of land, though, where a colt could disappear without leaving any more of a trace than the people.

It was a long morning. I came back to the ranch about noon with Clay and two other horses, and Charles was waiting right there on the porch where I'd left him. His face, when he saw I didn't have the colt, got a little tighter-looking.

"Didn't you even see Alado?" he asked.

"No."

He paused, swinging one foot out over the steps. "Would you tell me if you had?"

He looked at me, and I knew he wanted to know if I had found the colt dead. I said, "When I find him, dead or alive, you'll know about it." And I saddled Clay and rode off again.

"Good luck, Uncle Coot," he called.

"Right."

By the end of the week he was still calling "Good luck" as I rode off, but luck was running out. I had gone over my ranch and most of the land beyond, and I had found every horse and colt but Alado.

I was keeping my eye on the sky now, watching for vultures more than anything else. I found myself thinking about a scene in an old movie called *The Red Pony*. In this scene vultures flew down and ate the dead pony. The way they did that was to tie strips of raw meat onto a dummy pony. Then they got some real hungry vultures and let them loose, and the vultures flew right down in front of the cameras and began to tear off pieces of flesh. It was a real-looking scene, and it kept flashing in and out of my mind as I rode.

By now I knew I wasn't going to find Alado. I figured he had died somewhere up in the mountains or drowned in one of the swift streams that form in the arroyos after a heavy rain. The only good thing about the situation was that Alado had been weaned, so he might not starve to death; that is, if he *was* still alive.

I kept looking long after I knew there was no hope, because in my own way I felt as bad about losing the colt as Charles did. Alado hadn't been my whole life, of course, the way he'd been with Charles, but I sure hated it that he was gone.

There was one other thing too. Charles had a lot of confidence in me, in the fact that I *would* find the colt. He kept saying over and over, "You'll find him. I know you will," and I could see he believed it. A couple of times I said, "Look, maybe I can find him, but more likely I can't, Charles."

He would always answer, "You can. Uncle Coot, you can do *anything*."

Finally, though, I had to give up. I didn't say anything, but one morning at the time I usually saddled Clay and went off, I started fixing the fence instead.

Charles came running out and cried, "Uncle Coot!"

I said, "What?" I looked at him but I didn't stop working.

"Aren't you going out to look for Alado?" He paused, and I couldn't see his eyes because the sun was shining on his glasses. To tell you the truth I was glad of it.

I stopped what I was doing and said, "Charles, look, I want to explain something to you."

"Aren't you going?"

I thought suddenly how I must have looked standing there—not a big man, dusty, scarred face, leaning to favor my bum hip. I wondered why he couldn't see me like I was. He had told me once the first time he ever saw me was in the movies, and I was leaping a forty-foot canyon. I reckon an impression like that stays with a boy.

I rubbed the scar on my cheek. "Now, listen to me, Charles," I said.

"Are you going or not?"

I paused and let my breath out in a low sigh. Then I said, "No."

He shifted and the glare left his glasses, and I could see his eyes then. They had a blank look as if he hurt too bad to understand what was happening.

"Charles, I'm not giving up because I don't *want* to find the colt. Don't think that. It's just no use. I've gone over every mile of ground ten times and—"

"You don't have to explain."

"If I thought there was any way in the world to get Alado back I would be out there every day. It's been over two weeks, though, and no trace of him. You're smart enough to know what that means."

He kept looking at me for a moment, and then he turned away. "Wait a minute, Charles, I'm not through." He stopped, but now he was looking at the mountains instead of me. I said, "If there was any way to get the colt back I would. Now that's the truth."

He didn't say anything.

I said, "I know what the colt meant to you, but you're too bright a boy to hope for the impossible."

"It's not impossible for you," he said in a low voice. He looked at me. His voice rose. "Anyway, you don't have any idea what the colt means to me."

I looked into his eyes. I thought of myself when I was ten years old, and my grandad, who I was living with, led my horse Sandy away and sold him. I ran after my grandad that day and struck him and tried to pull the rope out of his hands, and finally they had to lock me in the corncrib. I can still remember yelling and throwing corncobs at that locked door.

Charles said, "Can I go now?" He started digging up dust with one foot. "I've got something to do."

Without waiting for me to nod, he started walking toward the house. I let him go. When I went in for lunch the first thing I saw was that all his notebooks and papers about Alado had been put away. The table where he kept them was cleared and pushed against the wall. The Polaroid pictures of me and him and Alado had been taken from the mantel.

I wanted to say something, but I couldn't find the right words. We sat down, ate, and I went back to work. Neither of us said much of anything for the rest of the week. And when we did start talking we just said things that needed saying like, "Pass the beans," or, "I need some help with the pump." Neither of us mentioned the colt.

Time kept passing and I kept thinking that things would get back to normal before long. But it didn't happen. I think Charles wrote his mom the first of September and asked if he could leave the ranch and go back East to school. I don't know for sure he did that—he wouldn't have told me about it anyway —but one day he got a letter from his mom that made him look like he didn't feel good.

I said, "Any news from your mom?"

"Nothing special," he said.

"How's her shoulder?"

"Fine. She'll probably be sending for me before long."

"Sure."

Without looking at me he added, "But I guess I'd better go ahead and start school here, just in case."

"Sure."

The canyon between us was wider than anything I ever jumped in the movies, and it would have taken a better stunt man than I ever was to get over it.

Something Wrong
at the Minneys' Again

It was the last of September and Charles was in school. This left me on the ranch alone now during the day, which was what I had wanted when Charles first came. But for some reason being by myself didn't make me feel as good as I had thought it would.

I was saddling Clay one morning when I looked up and saw Mrs. Minney's truck coming up the road. It was about nine o'clock in the morning, and she was moving like a freight express. The cloud of dust behind her shot straight up in the air and stayed there.

The truck made a half turn in front of the house, skidded in the dust, and came to a stop. I could see that Mrs. Minney was really upset this time, because it took her four tries to get the door open.

I hurried over and said, "Let me do that for you,

Mrs. Minney." I put out my hand and she struck at it through the open window.

"Don't you touch my door!"

I drew back and waited. She tugged the handle around and finally kicked the door open with her foot. Then she got out of the truck and stood looking at me without saying a word. Her face didn't have any more give to it than hardened dough.

I thought about this black steer my grandad used to have that got bogged down in a quicksand stream once. My grandad and me tried to pull him out, but we couldn't. He was stuck too deep. There wasn't any danger of him sinking lower and drowning though, so we left him overnight and came back the next morning with the mules. We knew in advance he was going to be mad because he was always bad-tempered, and standing overnight in quicksand wasn't going to improve him any. We roped him, pulled him out with the mules, and cut him loose. When he got to his feet he stood there glaring. Right before he started after us his eyes were as savage as anything you ever saw in your life. They looked a lot like Mrs. Minney's eyes right now.

Mrs. Minney reached out her finger and poked me in the chest. "You ought to be whipped," she said.

"What?"

"Whipped!" she shouted. "You ought to be whipped and run out of town."

"What are you talking about, Mrs. Minney?"

"You think you can get away with anything, treat people and animals any way."

"I don't know what you're talking about."

"Huh!"

"No, I really don't."

"Ho!"

"Mrs. Minney, if you'd just calm down and explain."

"Ha!" By this time she had me backed up against the side of the house, and her finger had almost poked a hole in my chest. I never saw such a mad woman. "You don't fool me," she said.

"But Mrs. Minney, I don't know what you're talking about. I really don't. You probably won't believe me, but I'm as dumb as that old horse over there." I pointed to Stump.

She looked from Stump to me. "At least," she said coldly.

I sighed. "Now just start at the beginning, Mrs. Minney, *please*."

She folded her arms and looked at me. Her eyes were real narrow. "Well," she said, "last night Frank and I went to bed early. He had been painting all day and I had been getting soil samples from caves and we were tired. It was about twelve o'clock and we were lying in bed, listening to the wind—did you ever hear such a wind? And then, just when the wind reached a peak, there was a terrible, ear-splitting crash on our tin roof."

"A crash?"

"The most terrible racket I ever heard. Mr. Minney and I sat up in bed and looked at each other. He said, 'Something's on our roof.' My heart stopped. We listened a minute more and he said, 'It's a cougar. A cougar has jumped onto our roof from the mesa and—"

"I have never seen cougar around here, Mrs. Minney," I interrupted. "It couldn't have been that. There are bobcats sometimes, but they wouldn't make a hard sound like you're describing."

"Don't try to be smart with me, hear? Frank heard the noise and he thought it was a cougar and I heard it and it sounded like a cougar to me too. You, who didn't hear a thing, are now becoming an expert on it."

"I'm sorry."

"Well, if you don't keep quiet, I'll just go into town and find the sheriff. I imagine he'll listen without giving me a lot of unnecessary talk about bobcats."

"I won't say another word."

She gave me a hard look before she continued. "So Frank said he would go and see if he could get the cougar off the roof, but I said, 'No, if anybody goes after the cougar, it had better be me,' and finally he agreed."

"I imagine so."

"I got the broom and the rifle and the flashlight and went out the back door. All this time there was such a clattering on the roof you wouldn't believe it." She began to wring her hands. "I was shaking like a leaf. I couldn't even push the button on the flashlight, Mr. Cutter." She began to wring her hands harder than ever. "And then the moon came from behind a cloud and I looked up on the roof and I dropped the flashlight *and* the rifle *and* the broom."

"What was it, Mrs. Minney?"

"Because there on my roof—" She broke off to get her breath.

"Yes, Mrs. Minney?"

"There on my roof—"

"Mrs. Minney, *what was on your roof?*"

She looked at me. "The winged colt." And when she said that, she reached out and poked my chest so hard I thought there would be a place left in my skin for the rest of my life, like a hole I have in my leg where a steer horned me.

"The winged colt?"

She nodded.

"But that couldn't be. Mrs. Minney, the colt was lost in a storm in August and we haven't seen him since."

"He was on my roof last night."

"But, Mrs. Minney—"

"He was on my roof last night, and as soon as I saw him I called Frank, and Frank said that one of us was going to have to climb up and carry him down."

I was so stunned I couldn't speak.

"What appeared to have happened, Mr. Cutter," she went on, "was that the colt was over on the mesa, and during the wind storm he got blown onto our roof. He was pathetic, scared as a rabbit. I said to Frank, 'Well, if anybody's going to climb up there it better be me since I've been climbing cliffs for two months now.''

"And he agreed."

She nodded. "So we got the ladder and I started up. A roof is not as pleasant a place as you'd think, I can tell you that. But I inched over to where the colt was and I grabbed. For some reason, Mr. Cutter, even though I slipped over easy as a snake, it scared him. And then—I tell you, Mr. Cutter, it makes my heart stop to think about it even now—and then those wings came out and the colt flew off the roof. It was awful. He flew to the ground and I, having no wings, just fell right off like a sack of grain and lay there for twenty minutes."

"And the colt?"

"He was fine. He landed about twenty feet from the house."

"Where is he now?" I said quickly. "Do you know?"

"By this time I was able to get up and go in the house," she continued. "I got an apple and came back and held it out to the colt. He came over in the light and he was pitiful, Mr. Cutter, half starved. I could count his ribs."

"But where is he *now*?"

"Later I said to Frank, 'I should think that man' —meaning *you*—'would take better care of his animals than this. I should think he would look after his colts and not let them fly all over the countryside scaring people out of their beds!' "

"Mrs. Minney, where is the colt *now?*" By this time I was ready to take her and shake an answer out of her, like my grandad did to me when I was a boy and got a nickel caught in my throat—just turned me up and shook until it plopped out in front of everybody in church. "*Where is the colt?*"

She looked at me. "The colt is in my barn." She held up one hand. "But before you come get him, I want some assurance that this sort of thing is not going to happen again. Frank and I need our sleep at night. We cannot be crawling up on roofs to get colts

in the middle of the night and then have them flying around the yard like birds."

"Yes'm." I wasn't going to give her an argument about anything now.

"And so I'm going to ask for your promise that this is not going to happen again."

"I promise."

She looked at me hard, and then she nodded. "I'm going to give you one more chance, Mr. Cutter. I just hope I won't regret it."

"You won't."

"Well, then, you can come get the colt this afternoon." She started walking back to the truck.

"Mrs. Minney, one thing before you go." She turned and looked at me. "Just thank you, Mrs. Minney, that's all."

"Huh!"

"No, I mean it. Charles has had a bad time over this. He cared a lot about that colt."

"Too much, if you ask me."

"Yes'm, and he sort of blamed me for what happened."

"Well, I should think so." She looked at me. "Of course it's none of my business, but that boy's mother ought to be taking care of him."

"I know that."

"An uncle is no substitute for a mother."

"Yes'm."

She looked at me again. I thought her eyes could

see all the way through me. "Still," she said, "I guess you're better than nothing."

"Well, I'm trying to be." She got into the truck and looked at me while she was turning the key. I said, "Thank you again, Mrs. Minney. I really mean it."

"Huh!" she said and drove off in a cloud of dust.

To Get a Colt

When Charles got home from school that day I was waiting for him by the truck. I said, "Put your books down and get in. We got an errand to do."

Charles set his books on the edge of the porch and got in the truck. "Where are we going?"

"To get a colt."

He didn't answer, just looked straight ahead at the road. I had offered Charles one of the other colts after Alado was lost, but he had said no. And I had sold the colts about a week ago.

"Why are you getting another colt?" he asked. "What kind is it?"

"Palomino."

He looked at me when I said that. "Palomino?" he asked in a funny voice. For a long time we had been real careful what we said to each other. Never once had we mentioned Alado. Even the word "Palomino" was out. Still, the colt had always been right beneath the surface of both our minds. Now it was out in the open.

"Palomino," I said again.

"Where is it?"

"Over at Mrs. Minney's. It got up on her roof last night, and she came over this morning all upset about it." I said this with a real straight face, and he looked at me and didn't say anything. "What she figured happened"—I went on—"was that the colt kind of got blown over from the mesa, carried by his wings, and—"

When he heard that, he grabbed me by the arm. "Is it our colt? Is it Alado?"

"Yeah."

"Is that the truth?"

"Yeah."

"Uncle Coot, is that the *real* truth?"

"*Yeah.*"

"Don't kid me, Uncle Coot. Is that the real *honest* truth?"

"Yeah, it is the real honest truth."

"I don't believe you."

We went on like that all the way to Mrs. Minney's. Finally, when we drove up in the yard and Charles saw Mrs. Minney standing there waiting for us with her hands on her hips, he began to believe.

"Where's the colt?" he asked. He got out of the truck so fast he went down on his knees in the dust.

He scrambled up and stood there. He looked like he'd stopped breathing.

"He's in the barn, young man, but I want to tell you one thing before we get him, the same thing I told your uncle. A colt is to be taken care of and not allowed to fly over people's houses in the dead of night."

"Yes'm. Can I—"

"If you can't take care of a colt, you don't deserve to have one."

"No'm, can I see him now?"

She gave both of us a good long look and then she said, "Come on," and led the way into the barn.

Alado was in the back stall, standing quietly, but as soon as he saw us, he started moving around. I said, "Stay back, Charles," because a colt can injure himself real easy in the first year of his life. You even have to be careful of a nail sticking out of the stall because a colt will just go wild sometimes. "Let's stay back." I took Charles by the arm and held him, because he was bent on running right into the stall and throwing himself on the colt.

He stayed but he didn't like it. We waited a bit, the three of us, while I talked to the colt and gradually we moved closer.

I had been feeling mighty good up until this point, but I got solemn fast. The colt was the sorriest sight I had seen in a long time, thin and shaky in the legs, and I could count all his ribs. It worried me. I'd seen it happen before. Colts that have a bad first year never make it up sometimes. They never recover the growth they've lost. You can sometimes spot a colt that's been neglected just by its shape, even when it gets older.

I took the halter I'd brought with me and stepped closer. We had been putting a halter on Alado from the time he was two weeks old. Now he shied and jumped backwards. I calmed him finally and got the halter on and led him out into the yard.

There's a way to lead a colt—you keep his shoulder against your leg or hip and never pull him behind you like a toy. Alado wouldn't stay with me though; he kept pulling away and shying, and it took us a while to get him in the trailer.

Just when we were ready to drive off, Mrs. Minney came to where I was standing by the truck. I said, "You don't have to say another word, Mrs. Minney. I am going to take the best care of this colt you ever saw," because I thought she was going to light into me again about the way we'd treated Alado.

Instead she shook her head and said, "You know, it's a funny thing, Mr. Cutter, but I thought I saw another animal with Alado last night up on the mesa. Could that be possible?"

"Another animal? I don't think so."

"But Mr. Minney got the same impression."

"Another animal *with* the colt?"

"Either with him or after him," she said. "We couldn't tell which."

Right then Charles called from the back of the truck. "Come on, Uncle Coot, Alado's getting restless."

"I'll be right there, Charles." I turned back to Mrs. Minney. "What kind of animal was it?"

"Mr. Cutter, I've told you all I know."

"Could it have been another horse?"

She shook her head. "Not big enough."

"A coyote?"

"I never saw a coyote. Now, Mr. Cutter, that is all I know."

"Are you coming, Uncle Coot?" Charles called.

"Right away." I got in the truck and backed around. On the way home I gave some thought to what Mrs. Minney had said, but when we got the colt in the corral, I forgot everything but his condition. He was pitiful, gaunt as a rail.

"He looks so bad," Charles said, leaning over the fence.

"I know." Alado was standing on the far side of the corral now. His energy, every bit of it, was gone. His wings had a droopy look to them as if they were too heavy to hold to his sides. His head was turned to the ground.

"Will he ever get strong again?" Charles asked. I knew it hurt him to see the colt in such a poor condition. It sure hurt me.

"Well, we'll do what we can," I answered. "We'll double his feed and put an egg in it and some butter. Before you know it, he'll be stronger than Clay."

"I hope so." Charles turned. "I'll go mix up some feed right now." He left and started whistling halfway across the yard. I stood there staring at the colt. I thought as I looked at him how very vulnerable he was. What an easy prey. I thought about what Mrs. Minney had said. Something was either *with* him or *after* him. If something was after him, he was there for the taking.

A White Form
in the Mesquite

I couldn't get to sleep that night, and so about midnight I went out on the porch, sat in a chair and put my feet up on the railing.

The Comanches called the month of September the Mexico Moon, and I always think of them late on a September night. They used to come through here on their way to Mexico to get horses. Every September they'd come when the nights were clear and mild. Their trail, a long pale ribbon from the buffalo plains down to Mexico, used to come right about where I was sitting.

While I was thinking about this I kept my eye on Alado over in the corral. His wings were still drooping, and the moonlight made them appear to be a load thrown over his shoulders. But then, I thought, maybe that's what they were—a burden.

I leaned back in my chair, crossed my legs, and

closed my eyes. The thing that kept flitting in and out of my mind was what Mrs. Minney had said that afternoon. Something was either with the colt or after him.

I couldn't make sense of it either way. First of all there wasn't much danger from animals around here any more. Years ago, a hundred and fifty or so, there were great grizzly bears in the mountains. They could travel forty miles a day, and meeting up with one meant death. Thirty years later, though, every one of them had been killed by hunters.

Even coyotes were scarce now. I remember my grandad telling me about the time he was out herding cattle, and coyotes kept pestering him and keeping him awake. My grandad didn't want to shoot because of the cattle, so he finally threw one of his boots at them. Next morning he found that the boot had landed in the banked embers of the campfire and been burned to a crisp. My grandad held the loss of that boot against the coyotes until he died.

A coyote was about the only thing I could think of that could be after the colt. Usually a coyote eats what it finds dead—gophers or jack rabbits, but it also kills stray sheep and calves on occasion. With the colt's weakened condition it could kill him. I sat there for the best part of an hour, but I still couldn't think of any animal that could be *with* the colt.

I dozed in my chair and awoke abruptly with my hands still folded over my chest. Something had awakened me, but I didn't know what. I leaned forward. I realized suddenly that I couldn't see the colt, and I got to my feet.

As I stood there I heard a high howling noise in the distance, and I felt a chill on the back of my neck. I went down the steps. "Alado!" I called.

I waited, listening. Suddenly the door slammed behind me, and Charles came rushing out. He almost ran me down. "What's wrong?"

"Probably nothing, Charles, but you better get my gun just in case."

"Your gun? What's wrong? Has something happened?"

"I don't know."

Without another word he went into the house, came back with my rifle, and put it in my hands. I said, "Now, stay behind me." We started walking toward the corral.

For a moment I couldn't see Alado at all, and then in the distance I caught sight of him. He had jumped the fence somehow, and he was running. There was nothing limp or weak about him now. It was a nervous, frenzied run, and Charles and I started after him.

As we crossed the yard, I heard the howl again. "Is it a wolf, Uncle Coot?"

"I don't know."

"What do you think?"

I had stopped thinking a long time ago. I said, "I'll get Clay."

Without taking time to saddle him I mounted

and started after Alado, my rifle in front of me. Charles shouted, "Wait for me, Uncle Coot, take me with you."

In the distance Alado was only a pale blur. The sound of the howling came again. "You wait here, Charles." I jabbed my feet into Clay's sides, and he set off in a gallop. He was a good range horse, quick and fast. You could turn him on a saddle blanket, and he was going like an arrow now, burning the earth.

He shortened the distance to the colt fast. We went out in front of Alado, circled and came back to head him off. Confused, Alado paused.

The howl came again—louder, closer. Alado threw up his head. Then he started forward, and I saw he was heading toward a mesquite thicket. I spun around and saw a low white form behind the mesquite.

I lifted my gun just in case. Alado moved between me and whatever was behind the mesquite. I waited. Alado whinnied and moved straight for the thicket.

I lowered my rifle. I knew Alado would not be running to meet danger. Slowly Clay and I moved closer. In the thicket ahead the white figure was crouched low. I knew now it couldn't be a coyote or a wolf.

I slipped off Clay's back and walked slowly toward the mesquite. I thought I knew now what it was. I whistled softly. "Here, boy." I held my gun ready, the safety off, my finger on the trigger, just in case. "Here, boy."

There was a pause. Alado was right at my side now, nervously marking time, moving as if he was being jockeyed for a race. He whinnied and tossed his head into the air. His mane brushed my hand.

"Here, boy," I said, my eyes on the thicket. "Here!" I waited.

And then out of the thicket came the thinnest, puniest, sorriest-looking dog I ever saw in my life. He came out on his belly, crawling, his body as low to the ground as he could get it.

I knelt. "Come here, fellow." The dog came within three feet of me and then thought better of it. He writhed with uncertainty. He twisted. He turned his back on me. He made two complete circles. I could feel his agony, his desperate wanting to come, and his fear.

"Here, fellow, it's all right." Beside me Alado was quiet. I snapped my fingers. "Here."

The dog untwisted. He looked at me, but he stayed where he was. I held out my hand. He took two steps and got close enough to smell my fingers. I could have grabbed him and pulled him to me, but I knew better. "It's all right, boy." He moved close enough to let me scratch his neck. I knew he wasn't going away after that.

"Good boy." I looked at Alado and down at the dog. The dog wasn't much more than bones, worse-looking even than the colt. I didn't know how and I probably never would, but he and Alado had somehow

come together in the past month. The dog was probably the reason Alado was alive.

I rose after a minute, said, "Come, boy," and
started walking. The dog hesitated, but he couldn't re-
sist. Somebody a long time ago had probably said that
to him. With his head down he slunk after me. Alado
watched, and then he started after the dog.

We went along like that, Indian style, until we
met Charles running toward us. He said, "What happened, Uncle Coot? Was there something out there?"

"Yeah," I said. "That."

Charles came closer. "What is it? A dog?"

"Yeah."

"But where'd it come from, Uncle Coot?"

"Beats me," I said. "Mrs. Minney told me this
afternoon that she'd seen another animal on the mesa
with Alado. I guess that's what it was."

"But how did they get together?"

"I don't know." I glanced back at the colt and
the dog. "I reckon we never will know exactly what
happened. The way I figured it is that some time after
the storm the colt found the dog or the dog found the
colt and they survived together."

"Maybe the dog was used to horses. Maybe he'd
looked after calves or colts before," Charles said.
"Anyway, we *have* to keep him, Uncle Coot."

I nodded. I'd decided that myself as soon as I saw
Alado following the dog. I said, "I think at last we're
going to be able to train Alado."

Charles glanced around. "With the dog?"

"Yeah. I may be wrong, but I've got the feeling I can get Alado to do what I want just by getting the dog to do it first."

We walked on, and when we got back to the house Alado followed the dog right into the corral.

"See that?"

Charles nodded. He watched them a minute, and then he glanced at me and grinned. "Too bad you can't teach the dog to *fly*."

"Yeah, that would be nice, wouldn't it?" Then I took a good easy breath, the first I'd drawn in months. "Well, we better feed the dog, I guess, and get to bed. Alado'll be all right now."

"I'll feed him, Uncle Coot," Charles said. He ran into the house.

I took one more look at the dog and the colt and I went in the house too. I fell asleep dreaming of the colt, not as he was, but as I wanted him to be, strong and sure and able to do anything.

$349 Worth of Snakes

For a while it seemed that my dream was going to come true, because throughout the winter Alado did get stronger and more sure of himself. Training him was easier with the dog, just as I'd hoped, and by spring Alado looked like a different animal. He was still wild, but there was a new certainty in his movements. I reckon he would have been like any yearling if it hadn't been for the wings. And so when we rode over to the butte one Saturday in May, there wasn't a thought in my mind of trouble.

There always have been a lot of snakes in this part of the country. My grandad told me that in 1926 some Mexican cotton pickers went after snakes one summer instead of cotton and five tons of snakes were turned in to the local dealers. My grandad said he made over thirty-nine dollars that year just in his spare time.

Snakes never worry me though. Generally a snake is a coward and a bluffer, and he'll hiss and rattle and give you every warning in the world before he strikes. The last thing I would have expected trouble from that day was snakes.

We had been riding for an hour or two, me in the lead, followed by Charles on Clay. Alado and the dog were trailing behind. The colt would step off to the side every now and then to investigate something or eat a little grass. Then he would run to catch up with us. A yearling is a beautiful frisky animal, and that was the way Alado was that day. Sometimes when you watch yearlings play and run you get the feeling that they think this is going to be their last free summer and they want to make the most of it.

Charles and I were over in the shadow of the butte, on the north side, and I heard a noise. It wasn't the sound a snake makes, but more of a steady buzzing, like bees swarming. I knew that snakes are generally attracted to buttes because of the crevices between the rocks, but I still hadn't thought about snakes.

I turned my horse toward the sound—I was curious—and Charles came with me. We rode slowly forward, coming up closer to the butte as we rode. Alado had left us and gone over into the brush, frisking and running on his own.

Since I was in the lead, I was the first to see what the noise was, and it stopped me cold. Dozens of rattlers were collected around a hole at the base of the butte. Since it was early May and hot, I figured the snakes were just coming out of their den because they were sluggish and didn't seem to have much life to them. That's the way snakes are when they first come out of hibernation.

"Well, did you ever see anything like that?" I asked Charles. I knew he hadn't because this was the first time I'd seen it myself.

Charles pulled his horse up beside mine, and both horses whinnied and moved backwards as soon as they saw the snakes. Horses are afraid of snakes and never get close to them if they can help it. In the movies when you see a horse trampling a snake under its hoofs, it's just a rubber snake. It looks real because the rubber snakes are built with a clock mechanism inside that causes the tongue to flick in and out. When they show a close-up of a real snake, they use fake horse legs. They never put the two together.

"Are they rattlers?" Charles asked.

"Yeah," I said. "There's nothing to worry about though. They haven't even started getting away from the den. They're still sleepy and sluggish from hibernation."

"Are you going to do anything about them?"

"Well, I'll probably get some dynamite later and blow up the den. One thing we don't need around here is a bunch of rattlesnakes."

"Rattlers are very dangerous," Charles said.

"Yeah."

I thought he was going to give me some facts and

information about the life and habits of rattlesnakes, but instead he shuddered. "You know, these are the first snakes I've seen in my whole life except in books."

"Well, it's a bunch of them." I rested in my saddle, leaning forward. I was thinking that with to-day's prices, those snakes might be worth about $349. I didn't feel much like collecting them and turning them in though. "We'll come back this afternoon, and you bring your camera and get some pictures before I blow it up."

The horses were still nervous, moving sideways and backwards, every way but forward where the snakes were. Charles and I kept looking. It was a real strange sight.

Just about this time I glanced up and saw Alado. I had forgotten about him because of the snakes, and when I looked up he was running straight toward us.

Sometimes a yearling will run as if he's in the greatest race of his life, and that was the way Alado was running. The only trouble was that the snakes were between us.

I turned my horse quickly and started around the snakes to head him off. I waved my hat and shouted, but this only made things worse, because Alado moved closer to the butte.

"Back, Alado," I shouted. The only way I could stop him now was to move right across those rattlers, and that was something I wasn't about to do. Rattlers can be sluggish, but they would liven up if a horse was trampling them.

"Alado, no, no!" Charles hollered. He tried to start Clay forward. I could see he was willing to ride right through the rattlers.

"Charles, get back!"

He heard me, but he kept urging his horse forward. I couldn't move for a moment, and then I shouted, "Stop, Clay, *back!*" Clay had been trampling the earth nervously, but he stopped at my command. "Back!" He turned, made a tight circle, and ran fifty yards in the opposite direction.

"Alado!" Charles cried. He was yanking the reins and doing everything he knew to get Clay turned around, only nothing worked.

Alado was coming so fast that he was on the snakes before he saw them. He had known something was wrong from the way Charles and I were acting. He had gotten nervous and skittish, and the fact that he didn't know what was wrong made him run faster. He was at top speed when he saw the snakes.

For a minute Alado acted like he was going to rear. He threw his head back, whinnied, and then he made a lunge forward as if he was trying to jump over the snakes, to clear them. He leaped into the air.

His eyes were wild. His mane was whipping the air. Everything in the world seemed to have stopped except this frenzied animal.

"Alado!" I cried. His wings came out then and beat down one stroke. Then there was another and another. "Alado!" I cried again, choking on the word. Alado was flying.

Flight

I've seen some terrible-looking things in my life. There's a beauty in a stunt that goes right—no matter how frightening it seems—and a sickening awfulness when one goes wrong.

That's what Alado's flight reminded me of, a stunt gone wrong, because I never saw anything wilder or more unnatural-looking in my life. I thought at the time that he would never get back to the ground alive.

His legs were moving in a sort of awkward, galloping motion, and then one of his wings brushed the side of the butte. This caused him to lose what balance he had, and his left wing dipped toward the ground.

Now he was fighting not only gravity, but being off balance. His wings beat harder, wild uneven strokes, and he rose a few feet. His hoofs were pawing the air with a certain desperation, as if it were a matter of climbing the air rather than flying through it.

Then it was over. In the last moment before his hoofs touched the ground, his body straightened. His wings stretched out. And he landed on all four hoofs, hard, like a bucking horse.

I was yelling at him by this time, yelling so loud my throat hurt, but he started running. It was as if he was being pursued.

I started after him. I wasn't trying to catch him, just keep him heading in the direction of the ranch, but we went for the best part of an hour before he slowed down. Then it took me another half hour to catch him and get a rope on him. He was just plain worn out then and I was too. After we rested he followed me home, gentle as a lamb.

I was with him in the corral, rubbing him down and talking to him when Charles rode up an hour later. Charles was so tired and saddle sore he could hardly get off his horse. I knew what a struggle he'd had trying to keep up with Alado and me because just ordinary riding wasn't easy for him.

"Are you all right?" I asked.

He didn't answer. He came running over. "Alado!"

"He's all right."

"I thought he was going to be *killed!*"

"Yeah, me too."

The struggle came into my mind, and the unnaturalness of what I had seen stunned me all over again. When you're training an animal, teaching him to do something unnatural like fall, you have to do it slowly. You have to build up to it. The difficulty here was that there had been no way to train Alado to fly. Flight was against his nature, and the whole experience had been one desperate attempt to get safely back to the ground.

Charles rubbed Alado's neck. After a minute he glanced over at me. "You shouldn't have tried to stop me," he said. He turned his face away and laid his cheek against the colt's neck.

"What?" I hadn't heard him good because his face was half-buried in the horse's mane.

He lifted his head. "You shouldn't have tried to stop me."

"Well, you shouldn't have tried to go through those rattlers. You talk about stupid things—now that *was* stupid. You could have been killed."

He didn't look at me. It was the first stirring of something, like the brewing of a storm, a change in the air. I wanted to smooth things over because both of us were tired and upset. "I'm going in," I said. I patted Alado on the rump and started for the house.

Charles said, "If you didn't want to save him— that's your business. Only you shouldn't have stopped me."

I turned around. "Is that what's wrong? You think I could have saved him?"

He looked at me. "If you'd cared enough."

I stood there for a minute. I didn't know what to say. There's not a man who has loved horses better than me. The first thing I ever loved was a horse. The first tears I ever remember shedding were over a horse and dried on a horse's neck. There have been a time or two in my life when a horse was the only friend I had in the world. I thought of Cotton. I realized suddenly I was rubbing the scar on my cheek. It had been a while since I'd done that. I looked at the mountains in the distance. Then I looked at Charles. His eyes were burning in his dusty face.

I still didn't know what to say. Suddenly everything was confused, beyond what I could understand. I said, "Just because a horse has wings, Charles, you can't—" I stopped in the middle because I realized that wasn't what I wanted to say at all.

"It isn't the wings," he said. "You don't understand anything. If he was a plain ordinary horse it would be the same to me."

The colt was quiet now, standing between us, letting Charles rub his neck. Charles was still looking at me. He wanted something from me, I knew that, but I didn't know what. Maybe he wanted a promise that the horse would always be safe. Maybe he wanted me to be the great, wonderful hero he had always thought I was.

We waited, standing there, and finally I said, "Just don't let yourself care too much about the colt. That's all." I turned away then and went into the house.

Late that afternoon I rode out with dynamite and

blew up the rattlesnake den. I told Charles he could come along, because I figured he would never have a chance to see something like that again, but he said he was too tired and wanted to stay home with Alado. I waited, taking a long time getting started because I thought he might want to change his mind. He didn't, though, and in the end I rode out by myself.

It was just as well he didn't come, I guess, because there wasn't much to see. There was just a dusty explosion and a lot of dead snakes. I rode around for a while to see if I could see any alive and wiggling, but I couldn't. Then I headed for home.

As I rode I found myself thinking of something Mrs. Minney had told me the other day. She told me she had been up in the mountains, and she'd found an old Indian grave. There was a skeleton curled up in it and the dust of some possessions—a bow and arrows, a blanket. No telling how long it had been there and no one knew about it. For some reason thinking about that brought my troubles down to size.

By the time I got back to the ranch I had started telling myself that Charles and I had just had a little quarrel, which was natural enough under the circumstances. I decided to forget it.

Charles and Alado were in the corral along with the dog when I got there. I said to the dog, "Well, where were you when we needed you?"

Charles grinned a little. "I think he was more scared than any of us. Did you kill the rattlers, Uncle Coot?"

I nodded. "Yeah, I got them all."

"Well, we shouldn't have any more trouble then, should we?" Charles asked. He asked it in such a hopeful way that I told him what he wanted to hear.

"No, we shouldn't have any more trouble."

More in the Sky Than Hawks

In this part of the country anything seems possible in the summer. The colors are brighter than any you ever saw and the bare mountains against the sky look like their names—Cathedral Point and Weeping Women and Devil's Back. A desert arroyo, dry for years, rushes with water after a rain, and the Marfa light burns in the desert and no one can find it. A winged colt doesn't seem strange at all in the Texas summer.

June started slow and easy. Charles was out of school now and spending most of his time with Alado. Mr. and Mrs. Minney had gone back East for a visit, leaving with us a painting of Alado flying off the roof of their house that night last September. We set the picture on the mantel, but neither Charles nor I liked to look at it. It showed too plainly what could happen. It made Alado's desperation, the danger of his flying very real, and most of the time we avoided it. Occasionally, however, I would come into the room and find Charles standing there staring at the picture, and occasionally he would come in and find me doing the same thing. We worried a lot in silence.

On this particular day Charles decided to take Alado to the mesa, which was about two miles behind the house. A mesa, which means "table" in Spanish, is just a flat-topped piece of land with steep sides. It used to be a hill, I guess, only the sides washed away and the top wore smooth, leaving a piece of land like a platform. There was a stream that ran by the mesa after a rain, and that was why Charles had decided to go.

Charles and Alado set out and right away the dog came crawling out from under the porch and started after them. He never liked Alado to go off without him.

The dog was still not much more than a skeleton. We had fed him enough for two dogs; we had given him better than we ate. Still he was bones, and that's what Charles called him. When Bones lay down on the porch it sounded like someone had dropped kindling wood.

At three o'clock I was outside working on the truck, and I happened to glance up and see a glider flying overhead. The glider was low, circling about a mile north of the corral. I straightened up quick.

"Hey, Charles!" I called, in case he had come home without my seeing him. "Charles!" I wanted him to see the glider because that was all he had been talking about since Sunday, when we had gone into Marfa. The National Gliding Championship was being held there, and since these were the first gliders Charles had ever seen, he couldn't quit talking about them.

A glider, in case you never saw one either, is an airplane that flies without an engine. These gliders have races and distance tasks, and when the contest is going on, you can see gliders and glider trailers everywhere you look.

Charles and I had gone to the airport on Sunday, and it was an awesome sight. Seventy gliders were all stretched out on the ramp, waiting to be towed up by airplanes. Later it was even more awesome to see them in the sky, seventeen or eighteen of them together, circling beneath the clouds.

A glider, I learned that afternoon, is a lot prettier than an airplane. The wings are real long and slender, and I reckon it comes closer than anything I ever saw to being a bird.

Well, we had gotten into the truck finally and started for home, but Charles couldn't talk about anything but gliders. He knew the name of every glider he'd seen—the Libelle and the Kestrel—and he knew that gliders go up by getting lift from air currents, and he knew what some of the altitude and distance records were. He told me that one of the gliders we saw had flown nonstop for six hundred miles.

Every day since then Charles had spent most of

his time outside squinting up at the sky, watching for gliders. He claimed a couple of times that he had seen one over the mountain peaks in the distance, but it had looked more like a hawk to me.

"Charles!" I called again. I knew he was going to be disappointed. After all that watching here was a glider practically over the corral, and he wasn't around to see it. There was a chance he'd seen it from the mesa, I thought, because the glider had come from that direction, but I wasn't sure.

I watched the glider and, from what Charles had told me, I figured that the pilot wasn't doing too well. He had gotten low and was moving from one place to another trying to find some lift so he could get high enough to finish the race.

I watched for a while, but it didn't look like he was getting any higher to me. The glider moved on toward the road. It was almost overhead.

I was getting excited now. In this part of Texas there aren't many places to land a glider because most of the land has yucca and mesquite on it. So sometimes—Charles had learned this at the airport—the pilots land their gliders on the road.

By now the glider was even lower and so close overhead I could hear a funny eerie noise as it passed, a whistling sound. The pilot moved closer to the road. He was really low now, and I got in my truck and drove as fast as I could. I got to the main road just in time to see the glider land.

I went over and helped the pilot pull his glider to the side of the road, and then I looked it over. The pilot leaned in the cockpit and did something to his instruments. Then he glanced at me. I was standing at the back of the glider, by the T-shaped tail.

"You own that ranch over there?" he asked.

I nodded. "What is this for?" I asked, pointing to a metal thing that was sticking out of the tail. And then the pilot asked something that stopped me cold.

He said, "What was that thing I saw flying back there at the mesa?"

"What?" I asked. My hand dropped to my side.

"Back there behind your place. I couldn't get a good look at what it was because I was trying to find some lift, but it was flying. It looked as big as a horse. I don't suppose you folks raise flying horses around here." He laughed.

I got a funny feeling in the pit of my stomach. I said quickly, "Look, if there's nothing I can do for you here, I better get back to the ranch." I knew that Charles was in trouble.

He said, "Sure, here comes my crew now." We looked up the road at a car pulling a long white trailer.

I said again, "I better get going."

I got in the truck and drove back to the ranch as fast as I could. I jumped out and saw Bones coming toward the house. He was just a streak he was going so fast, and his tail was between his legs and his ears were flattened against his head. He ran around the house and went under the steps. I heard him work his way back under the porch where there was a break in the stones. He was wheezing and panting as if his lungs would burst.

"Come here, Bones."

The wheezing and panting stopped. Even the breathing seemed to have stopped.

"Come here, Bones, *come.*"

As soon as the pilot had mentioned seeing something fly back at the mesa I had known something was wrong. It was confirmed now. Unless something had happened to frighten him badly, the dog would never have left Alado.

Clay was already saddled. I started out as fast as I could in the direction Charles and Alado had taken. I rode all the way to the mesa without seeing a trace of them.

"Charles! Charles!"

There was no answer. I turned Clay and rode to the right. I had the feeling that something had happened to Charles, and I suddenly got a sickness in my stomach. It was like that time with Cotton, only worse. I thought I might fall out of the saddle.

I rode, stopped, and called again. "Charles, where are you?" I threw back my head and bellowed, "*Charles!*"

I waited a minute, and then I heard his voice in the distance. I rode around the mesa.

"Here I am," he called.

I looked up and saw Charles clinging to the side of the mesa. He hadn't gotten far, and he appeared to be stuck.

"What are you doing up there?" The relief of seeing him safe made me yell louder than was necessary.

"Uncle Coot?" He hadn't been crying, but he was stammering so badly I could hardly recognize my own name.

"What happened?"

"Uncle Coot?"

"What *happened*?" He swallowed and I said, "Now, come on, Charles, what are you doing up there? What's going on?"

"I don't know exactly," he said, still stuttering a little.

"Well, try to tell me what happened. Start at the beginning."

"We were coming down to the stream, me and Bones and Alado, just like we planned."

He stopped and I said, "Go *on*, Charles. The three of you were coming to the stream."

"Yes, and just then I looked up and saw a javelina ahead with her babies."

"Go on." A javelina is a wild pig. They can be mean, but there's not much danger as long as you let them alone. "You didn't bother them, did you?"

"No, as soon as I saw them, I started backing up. I was going around to the other side."

"So what happened?"

"Well, when I stepped back, I stepped right on Bones. He was behind me, see, and as soon as I did this, he let out a terrible howl and leaped forward and landed directly in front of the javelina." He paused and shook his head. "After that I just don't know what did happen. It was like a tornado. Pigs were charging— it seemed like there were a hundred of them—and Bones was howling and running—and I was trying to grab Bones and we all rolled right into the path of Alado."

"And Alado flew," I said with a sinking feeling.

"It was terrible at first, Uncle Coot. I was never so scared in my life. And then all of a sudden he was flying. It wasn't like at the snake den. He was *really* flying."

"Well, that's great." I knew there was something that he hadn't told me yet. "If Alado can get control of himself, he'll be safe," I said, sort of marking time. "We won't have to worry about him."

"I thought he was never going to stop, Uncle Coot. He flew and flew and *flew*."

Suddenly a terrible thought came to me. I said slowly and carefully, "Where is Alado now, Charles?"

At that question Charles's face sort of crumpled.

"Where is he now?" I asked, hitting at every word.

Charles swallowed.

"*Where is Alado?*"

Without a word Charles lifted one hand. He pointed to the top of the mesa. With a sort of sick feeling in my stomach I looked up and saw standing on top of the mesa, about fifty miles above us—anyway that was how it looked—the colt Alado.

Those Who Can—Fly

Charles raised his head, and we both looked up at the colt for a moment. The height gave him a frailness, and Charles looked away quickly. He said in a rush, "But he flew real good, Uncle Coot. I wish you could have been here. He really flew!"

"I can see that."

"I mean he can really *fly*, Uncle Coot. He—"

"I can see that, Charles. There's no other way he could get up on top of that mesa."

There was a moment of silence, and then Charles said, "How are you going to get him down?"

All at once I felt tired. I suddenly thought of the early days of movie gags. The stunt men never used to look real in their falls. They would gallop up at top speed, bring their horses to a halt, and *then* fall out of the saddle. I felt like that was what was going to happen to me now. I had come galloping up as fast as I could, and now suddenly I felt so tired I could have just dropped out of the saddle.

It was Charles's last statement that did it, I think, that "How are *you* going to get him down?"

I sighed. I realized that maybe it wasn't that I felt tired. It was that I felt just like what I was—a man with a lot more than his share of scars and a lot less than his share of brains. I was aware of my bum hip and my scarred cheek, my gored leg, my twice-broken wrist. The years of knocking around rose up and hit me all over again while I was sitting there.

Charles said again, "How are you going to get him down?"

"Well," I said finally, "I reckon he'll have to get down the same way he got up." To tell the truth I didn't know what to do about the colt. The sight of him up on the mesa had made me feel like I'd had too much sun.

"You mean fly down?" he asked.

"Yeah, I guess he'll have to fly down."

"But, Uncle Coot, he only flies when he's startled or frightened. He would never just fly on his own. He can't reason that out. You told me yourself that horses can't reason."

"Well, some horses can probably reason," I said. "I'm no expert."

"You told me that horses do foolish things sometimes because they can't reason. I remember you saying this at the table one night, like horses will run straight into a fire instead of away from it."

"But flying is an instinct with this horse."

"I *know* he won't fly down."

"Well, we can wait and see, can't we? We don't have to start risking our lives this second." I wanted some time, but I could see I wasn't going to get it.

"You can wait if you want to." Charles started scrambling up the side of the mesa. His position hadn't been good to start with, and what with all the sliding and slipping he ended up even lower than he had started. He looked at me and said, "Don't try to stop me." And he started up again.

I stayed where I was. When Charles had slipped a second time I said, "Now, look, Charles, don't get in such a hurry. Why don't we—"

"I'm not going to wait around for him to fall off and kill himself. I don't care what you do." He was still making climbing motions, but he had worn through the legs of his pants and skinned both his knees, and that was slowing him down some. He said again, "There's no need your trying to stop me." This time he said it like he was trying to give me an idea.

The last thing in the world I wanted to do was get off my horse and climb that mesa, particularly when I didn't know what to do when I got up there. I sat a minute more, leaning forward on my saddle. I shifted, and then before I could say anything Charles blurted out, "You don't care about Alado at all, do you?"

It caught me by surprise, the way he said it and the way he was looking at me. "What?"

"You don't care about Alado." He paused. "You don't care about anything."

"Wait a minute now," I said. "I care about the horse."

"You didn't want to get him that night in the storm."

"The night I almost killed myself going after him? That night? I'm not Superman, you know, I'm just—"

"You didn't want to go that night and you didn't want to look for him after the storm, and then that day at the rattlesnake den, you—"

"Now, just hold on a minute," I hollered. He shut up because my voice had gotten loud as thunder. I wanted to say something then—he was listening— but for some reason I froze. All my life I've been troubled by not being able to say what I wanted.

He waited, and the moment for me to speak came and went. He said, "You don't care about anything," in a low voice. Then he added, "Or anybody."

Suddenly I remembered when I was six years old and I came galloping across the front yard on old Bumble Bee, standing up, arms out, yelling like an Indian. "Pa, look at me!" Later, when I hit the ground and lay there half dead, my pa came over and started pulling my belt to get the air back in me. He said, "You want to get yourself killed? Is that what you're trying to do?" It was the first summer I had seen my pa since I was a baby, and I wanted him to notice me so bad I would have tried about anything. Every time I got near him I'd put his hand on my head or his arm over my shoulder or I'd try to climb on his back or swing on his arm. I broke my wrist two times that summer trying to make him show he cared about me.

I said, "I'll go up and get the colt."

Charles wiped his nose and climbed down a few steps. I turned my horse to the right. For some reason I felt like my insides had been churned up with an egg beater.

Charles slid the rest of the way to the ground. He said, "How will you get him down?"

"I don't know." I rode Clay all the way around the mesa until I found a place where I might, with a lot of luck, be able to climb up without killing myself.

Charles came running over, out of breath. "Is this where you're going up?" he asked, squinting at the mesa.

"This is where I'm going to *try* to go up, yes."

"You can make it. I know you can."

I never felt less like a superman in my life. I said, "The cameras are not rolling now, Charles." I got off the horse and slung the reins over a bush.

Charles paused, and then he came over and rested one hand on Clay's neck. He hesitated. He said, "Maybe we could wait a little while, Uncle Coot. What do you think? Maybe he *will* fly down."

I started up the side of the mesa without saying anything. I'm not much of a climber. My bum hip bothers me when I have to put a lot of weight on it, and I slipped twice before I went ten feet.

"Uncle Coot, if you want to wait for a little while it's all right with me."

I kept going. I managed to get about halfway just by going real slow, one step at a time, the way a little kid goes up stairs. I stopped to rest against an outcropping of rock. "Are you doing all right?" Charles called from the ground.

"Wonderful."

"You look like you're almost a fourth of the way to the top."

I had thought I was bound to be a good bit farther than that, but I didn't say anything.

"The rest of the way looks like it's going to be a little harder though," he called. "It's steeper and there don't seem to be as many bushes to hold on to."

So far the total number of bushes I had found was one prickly-pear cactus which I would not advise holding unless it was a life-and-death situation. I rested a moment longer, and I started thinking how much easier things are in the movies. Like sometimes in a movie when somebody is supposed to be climbing up a cliff, they will just let him crawl on his stomach on the ground, and they will film this at a steep angle to make it look like he's climbing. Or when they're filming a sand storm, they throw stuff like talcum powder up in front of big fans and let that blow on the actors.

"Why are you stopping, Uncle Coot?" Charles called up. "Is there any special reason?"

The hurting in my hip had begun to ease. I looked down at him. "No, nothing special." I started climbing again.

I can't tell you exactly how long that climb took me, but it seemed like the longest afternoon of my life. And all the while Charles was calling things about my progress. He couldn't seem to shut up. Once I guess he looked away, because he called, "What happened? Did you slip?"

"Slip?"

"Yes, I thought you were farther up than that."

"No," I said, "I'm not any farther than this."

"Well, it just seems like you're lower now than you were, Uncle Coot."

"Lower in spirits," I said.

"What?"

"Nothing!"

"What? I couldn't hear what you said."

"*Nothing!*"

He must have known from the way that "nothing" rumbled down the side of the mesa that it would be a good idea for him to shut up. He didn't call to me any more, just gasped once when I did slip a little. I looked down at him right before I pulled myself up on top of the mesa, and he was standing there with his hands raised against his chest like a small church steeple.

The top of a mesa isn't anything beautiful—just some dry grass and rocks and a few straggly plants, but it looked good to me. I lay there on my stomach for a moment and then I stood up. My hip was hurting so bad I thought I wouldn't be able to walk. I shook my leg a little, which sometimes eases it, and tried to put weight on it.

Across the top of the mesa Alado was standing watching me. "Here, boy," I said.

He came over slowly, tossing his head. He had the reluctance any animal has in a strange situation, and he shied away a few times before he came. I patted him and scratched his nose. "When you fly, boy," I said, "you really fly, don't you?"

"Hey, Uncle Coot?" Charles called from below.

"What?"

"Is he all right?"

"Yes."

"He's not hurt or anything?"

"*He's* not."

"Are you sure?"

"Yes."

"Well, how are you going to get him down? Have you got any ideas yet?"

"No."

"As soon as you get an idea will you let me know?"

"Yes."

I looked at the colt and I scratched his nose again. "Alado," I said, "we are stuck." Then I shook my leg and rubbed his neck and tried to think of some way to do this impossible thing before dark.

Those Who Can't -Walk

The sun gets the color of desert poppies at sunset out here, but this evening it was something I dreaded seeing. I had been stuck up on the mesa with the colt for three hours, and I was no closer to getting him down than I had been at first. I was also bone tired and hungry and I did not have an idea in my whole head.

When I first got up I had tried to startle Alado a few times by waving my arms at him and tossing my hat under his feet. All I got for my trouble was a crumpled hat. The thing was that Alado wouldn't get near the edge of the mesa. As long as Charles and I had both been on the ground he had looked over constantly, coming right to the edge. Now that I was up here with him, he stayed in the exact center.

I didn't blame him really. If he went over the side, he wouldn't have to fall far before he struck the rocks, and it turned me cold to think about that. Still,

if he got a good running start, I kept thinking—
Then I would give him the old hat under the feet a
few more times. Nothing doing.

After a while I sat down and picked up little
pebbles and tossed them at a weed. Sometimes when
I'm doing something like that my mind works better,
but this time it didn't help.

"Uncle Coot?" Charles called from below.

"Yes."

"Are you still there?"

I sighed and bombarded the bush with every
pebble in my hand. "Yes, I am still here."

"Well, what are you doing?"

"Thinking."

He paused and then yelled, "What are you thinking *about*?"

What I was thinking about was those chutes they
used to build in the early days of movies, tilted over the
edge of a cliff and greased. The chutes were hidden so
they wouldn't show on the film, and once a horse got
started down the chute he couldn't stop. He would
have to go off the cliff. They got a lot of good pictures
that way, but a lot of ruined horses. In my mind I had
sent Alado down that greased chute half a dozen
times. "I'm not thinking of anything, Charles," I
yelled back.

"Well, if you do think of something—"

"Yeah, I'll let you know."

It stays light a long time out here—sunset is
usually about nine-thirty—but once the sun drops it

gets dark fast. By this time the sun was disappearing below the horizon. I got up, went to the edge of the cliff, and called: "Charles!"

His head almost snapped off his neck he looked up so fast. "What is it, Uncle Coot?"

"I want you to take Clay and go on back to the house, hear?"

"I don't want to."

"Well, do it anyway. There's no need both of us spending the night out here."

"I don't want to leave Alado," he said. "If you could only go ahead and get him down, then we could all go home together."

"Yes, that's true."

He looked down at his feet and then back up at me. He said, "I don't want to leave you either."

Sometimes a man's life shifts in a moment. It's happened to me more times than most men because I've had a hard fast life. I felt it happening again.

"Did you hear me, Uncle Coot? I don't want to leave you out here either."

I nodded. We kept standing there and I knew somehow that Charles, looking up at me on top of the mesa, seeing me from that distance, suddenly noticed how little separated us. I wasn't so much of a superman at that moment, and when I looked down at him, I could have been looking back over the years at myself. The truth slithered up to us like a sidewinder. Separated by the height of a mesa, we were the closest we had ever been.

"All right," I said, "go home, then, and get yourself a blanket."

"Thanks, Uncle Coot." He untied Clay quickly and rode off toward home. I watched till he was out of sight. Then I lay down, put my hat under my head, and tried to get some rest.

"I'm back, Uncle Coot," he called after a while.

I got up, walked to the edge of the mesa, and watched him spread out his blanket in the moonlight.

"I'll be right here if you need me."

"Fine, Charles."

I went back and lay down. There's no getting comfortable on top of a mesa—I had already found that out—but I got settled for a long night the best I could.

Alado was standing near my feet. He was so still I thought he must be asleep. About midnight—although I didn't think it would ever happen—my eyes closed too.

I woke up and it was two o'clock in the morning and I couldn't see the colt. I got up slowly. My hip had stiffened while I was asleep, and I limped forward a few steps.

I whistled and called: "Alado!" The sky was as bright with stars as I'd ever seen it and the moon was big. I looked around and I still couldn't see the colt. "Alado!"

For a moment there was silence and then I heard a whinny to my right. I hobbled over and saw what had happened.

On this side of the mesa there was a gentle slope.

At the bottom of the slope was a steep cliff, straight down to the rocks, but the colt didn't know this. The moonlight made everything look different, and I could see why he had been fooled. The colt had seen the slope, started down, and now he couldn't get back up.

"Here, Alado, come."

I reached down to take his halter and lead him back. Sometimes all a horse needs is a familiar hand to help him do something he couldn't do on his own. As I reached down, though, my hip gave way. It just buckled.

I yelled, more with surprise than pain, and then I slipped down the slope. I hollered and scratched and grabbed at whatever I could find. I went wild for a moment. I knew that if I didn't stop I would slip right off the cliff, take the colt with me, and both of us would end up on the rocks below.

My fingers dug into the ground like steel hooks, but I kept slipping. I was right by the colt's legs now, and although I hadn't touched him, he started slipping too. He was scared, I knew that, and for a moment I thought we were both lost. I squirmed around to avoid hitting him, and right then my foot found a rock ledge and I stopped.

"It's all right, Alado. It's all right, boy," I gasped.

He whinnied now, a loud high whinny. I turned over on my back and looked up. His pale legs were flashing by my face, thumping against the earth. Alado wasn't slipping any more, but the dirt was still sliding down the slope and over the cliff, and that gave him the feeling he was. I tried to reach up and hold him, but at that moment his wings flashed out. The wind from them beat against me. I drew back.

Alado paused a moment, the wings lashing at the air, covering me when they came down. It was a strange, eerie thing. The wings blocked out the sky, the whole world. I couldn't move and I couldn't speak. The colt slipped again. I was frozen against the ground. Then he slid a few more inches down the slope, and he was in the air.

I managed to sit up then and look down the cliff. For a second the colt seemed to drop straight down. He just sank. The huge white wings flashing in the night seemed powerless. His body was turned a little sideways. It was like a fever dream. Then, at the last moment, just when I thought he was going to crash into the rocks, an updraft of wind rose beneath his wings and he flew.

He flew away from the cliff, his pale wings powerful now, sure. This was the way I had dreamed he would fly. I couldn't move for a moment and it wasn't my hip either. It was the sight of that colt in the air. In all my life I have never seen anything like that, terrible and awesome at the same time. It was something that was going to be with me the rest of my days.

Then Alado landed about two hundred yards away and, without a break, ran off into the night.

I stayed there a moment, hanging on the slope like a kid halfway down a sliding board. I was still too caught up in what I'd seen to move. Finally I made

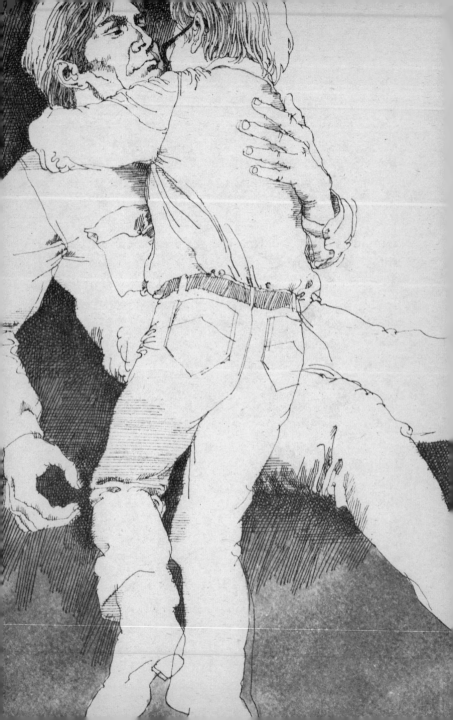

myself turn and work my way back up. I limped over, picked up my hat and put it on my head.

Then I stood there. I knew how Mrs. Minney felt that night on the roof when Alado went flying off, however badly, and she fell to the ground like a sack of grain. I hitched up my pants and started down.

I've heard men say that coming down a mountain is harder than climbing up, but it wasn't for me. After I climbed down the first part, which was red rock, I slid down the rest of the way—or fell sitting down, whatever you want to call it. I was rolling down the last part when Charles ran up and threw himself on top of me. It stopped me from rolling anyway. I

hesitated a minute, and then I put my arms around him and he started crying. He didn't make any noise doing it, but I knew he was crying because his tears were rolling down my neck.

"It's all right, Charles. It's all right." I patted him on the back.

He said, "You could have been killed."

For some reason his seeing me as I was, just a plain person, made me feel like crying too. I patted his back again. "It's all right." I waited until he was through crying, and then I said, "Did you see Alado?"

He nodded against my chest.

"You saw him fly?"

"Yes."

We stayed there a minute. "It was something, wasn't it?" I said.

"Yes."

"It was really something." I took a deep breath and slapped him on the back. "Well, let's get Clay and start for home." I could see when I raised up that Clay had walked over to the stream for a drink.

"I'll get him." Charles went running over to Clay and grabbed at the reins. He didn't get them on the first try, and the horse turned and trotted away a few steps. He looked at Charles. Charles went running at him again, and this time Clay turned and took off in the direction of home.

"Clay!" I yelled, but he was gone.

Charles came back slowly. He shrugged. "I don't know what I do wrong with horses."

I grinned a little in the dark. I said, "Give me a hand up." He helped me to my feet and I dusted myself off, and we started walking home.

Charles said, "I never will be the master of a horse, I know that now." He shook his head. "Never."

"You know what the Comanche used to do, don't you?"

"No."

"He used to find a wild mustang and rope him and throw him, and then he used to put his mouth over the horse's nose and breathe into it. He believed he was putting the controlling spirit into the horse."

"Well, I've tried everything else."

We heard the sound of a horse coming toward us and I said, "Well, old Clay's coming back. We'll be riding home after all."

I tell you it made me feel a lot better to think of easing myself up on Clay's back. Instead, when I looked, I saw Alado coming toward us. Alado went to Charles and nuzzled him and started walking beside him. I said, "It doesn't look like you're going to need that old Comanche trick after all."

"Maybe not." I could feel he was smiling a little.

We kept walking. It was slow because of my hip. I looked at the colt and the boy. I said, "I'll tell you something, Charles. One day that colt is going to fly as easy as he walks."

Charles looked at Alado. Without glancing back at me he said, "I know." I knew he was seeing again the pale wings in the dark sky just as I was. Seeing the colt fly like that, being the only two people in the world to have shared that awful and beautiful sight, touched us so much we couldn't speak of it any more. I knew he was thinking as I was, "One day—"

Suddenly I heard the sound of Clay's hoofs in the distance. "Clay," I shouted, "get over here." The sight of that horse coming out of the darkness was one of the best of my life. I limped to meet him. "Am I glad to see you, boy." I lifted myself into the saddle. Then I turned.

"Here, Charles, take my hand." I pulled him up behind me. "Let's go home." And we rode off together with Alado following behind.